A Cat Whisperer

By

Deborah Denise

A Cat Whisperer

Copyright 2018
by
Deborah Denise

Published by Ruskras Corner
The United States of America

ISBN- 978-1-942542-14-8
TX0009216818

Cast of Characters

Debriah Brock, legal age 27; A dark haired beauty, she had known loss in love. Her true nature conflicts with her beliefs in a way that is irreconcilable in the present era, making her prey to secrecy and seclusion. Nevertheless she finds satisfaction in her career and new joy in life upon finding love again.

Samantha Speer, legal age 27; A raven haired ingénue, her mission in life is to advance the cause of a vampire-free world. Not realizing her natural attractiveness, she never thought true love could happen to her. And when she had her first experience with the male exterior, it is fraught with danger and denial.

Raize Parks, legal age 47; Attractive for his age, his past holds a dire secret making him susceptible to blackmail in his powerful position as a police detective captain. He has sacrificed for years for his job and when true love arrives he finds he can give no more. He decides to take what life has offered him and damn the consequences. A new approach to detecting will prove as successful as his former techniques.

Marlotta Holt, legal age 36; Her husband's adulated profession gives her a place at the height of the social scale. However, she has her own lucrative career in a clandestine setting where prestige is carelessly tossed aside and reverence for the rule of law lost. She has no qualms about exploiting her success.

Lars Holt, legal age 36; His profession is the most honored in America, indispensable to the modern way of life. It allows him to live an independent existence unquestioned by his family or friends. However, he jeopardizes his marriage, position, and existence for a great tragic illegal love that cannot last.

Magdalene Rene Watters, age 16; she is a free spirit unaware of the dangers of love but she feels a duty to not let her lover take the entire blame if they are caught in their illegal passion. The hopelessness of the situation is mercifully unknown to her.

3

Bonita Holt, age 15; An ambitious soldier, she comes to see the military is not the only way to make her fortune and her parents are not who they say nor the family business is not what she was told. She fears she is a vampire and that predisposition might be trouble.

Loyce Landers, legal age 27; An undercover cop posing as a nude male dancer at The Men Unadorned Club, his adventure may lead to a second career, the love of his life, or death at the hands of evil.

Electra Simpson, legal age 50; Top FBI agent, she is one of the few with access to real time information in this era of privacy and intellectual rights. And she is the perfect mate for Raize Parks in this era of legal mating. She intends to marry him no matter what the consequences are nor how much harm is done.

Amy Raxel, legal age 40; Quiet, unassuming, the extremely efficient manager of The Male Unadorned Club is usually in the background. People tend to forget her instantly. While no angel by any definition, her redemptive value is her love and respect for her cat and dog, her only sources of love in her life.

Carlotta Fortune, Death Option at legal age 36; An icon, revered by all. Famous actress, a martyr to the Death Option cause, her premature demise to advance her career makes her forever a cult figure. Many fans cannot believe she is gone for eternity, especially now that scientists have proven life after death.

Earl Watters, undetermined age; A remnant of a past where it was legal for private citizens to have computers, he recalls the times when DVDs were not banned and cats did not talk openly to whisperers…

Earlene Watters, undetermined age; A sweet fluffy old lady with pin curls in her gray hair, she evokes an era from the past where gentleness was met with respect. She has had to hide her feelings for cats for many years.

Carousel, age confidential; Traumatized kitty witness to brutality, she keeps her wits about her and manages to land on her feet while humans around her are in turmoil.

4

The United States of America
Year- 2127

Not that far off!

Chapter 1

A sublime nap interrupted by two people in love.
The feline's eyelids flickered. Pupils enlarged.
Visiting?
Or trespassing?
No one should be here…
Unspoken subliminal observations…
Both male and female could not keep the cat from consciousness as they quickly undressed one another, caressing each other's skin, drinking in one another's blossoming scents.
Wide awake now, the kitty sniffed hard.
The man was wondering on the periphery of his mind where the animal had come from.
The girl reflected only that the calico was lovely.
Bliss soon took the place of observation and curiosity.
It was hot. The air conditioning was off. A glowing chandelier added heat.
The couple perspired in pleasure as they intertwined all possible parts of their bodies and in one motion sank down on the luxurious wide couch.
The feline nonchalantly bounded down from her perch on a bookcase to an arm of the sofa, distracting the man.
But the girl's adoring eyes never left her beloved's face.
Deciding his daughter must have brought the kitty home without asking, the man forgot the cat in an instant as he gazed into his girlfriend's brown eyes. His healthy physical desire for her engulfed him and he grabbed her behind, pulling her upward.
He thrust forward.
She also forgot the cat.
Gasping with pleasure as her lover pulsated deep within her interior, she vibrated in ecstasy with him.
In what seemed like just seconds it was over.
Knowing how rare the experience, they were still and solemn, their slim figures cutting slight indentions into the wide hard cushions.

Their bodies still near but no longer joined.

The cat jumped on top of them. They both laughed.

He grabbed the cat, and stood up, then dropped back down.

She remained stretched out on the sofa. Her legs under his buttocks. She moved them slightly, hoping skin friction would arouse him again.

The man clutched the feline, its fur threading within his chest hair. He petted it absentmindedly.

He sighed deeply. "I'd better dress. I have to leave soon."

She frowned.

"What did you tell Marlotta?"

The kitty meowed.

The young girl reached up and wiggled her fingers.

"Give," she said.

He handed her the cat.

"What did you tell your wife?" she insisted, affecting a slight pout.

He was spared from having to answer.

The chandelier appeared to shimmer. Abruptly the lights went out.

She let the cat go.

"Why is it so dark in here? It's nearly dusk outside," the girl fretted. "Get the lights back on right now."

"There's light-blocking shades and heavy curtains on the windows. And I don't dare open them. The neighbors spy."

"Then get the lights back on. I'm terrified of the dark."

"I'm trying to get dressed." The man flicked a cigarette lighter, looking for his clothes. "Let me get my clothes on. I'll flip the breaker switches."

"And it is not that I am afraid of the dark because I'm 16. I've always been and always will be and it has nothing to do with age."

Both were sensitive to her age. He was twice 16 plus 4.

Married with a child.

But they loved each other so.

A rare physical and emotional love.

They both knew it and neither knew what to do about it.

The consequences of being caught were so enormous they never spoke of it. The affair had been going on for months.

They both knew they would love until death.

The man held his clothes but did not dress. He pondered what to do about the breaker, which was mounted outside.

He had several nosy neighbors who would report any sight of him at home during this time of day to his wife.

"I'm scared," the girl repeated.

"Here, take this lighter and go upstairs to my daughter's room. Her curtains are always open. It will be brighter in that bedroom."

The man picked up a second cigarette lighter on an end table.

Cigarettes were made illegal more than 50 years ago but the lighters had become collectible and his wife was a registered collector, allowing her to possess auxiliary accessories made obsolete when related products were outlawed. She had bought several at an antique show.

True to her nature, she had carelessly left them about, losing interest in them as soon as she got them home.

His eyes followed the girl's light go steadily up the steps. She also did not bother to dress, but had taken her pants and shirt in hand.

As she disappeared, he debated again what to do.

He was not even sure he should dress yet. His uniform with its distinguishing hat was a dead giveaway. He could leave off the hat but that was no real solution.

Then his face might be visible.

He tried to recall if he had anything in his personal closet that would disguise his appearance.

He could not remember. Panic was setting in and he could not picture anything hanging from his coat hangers to save his life.

He merely recalled owning a lot of clothes. His was one of the highest paying professions in the nation. Before finding true love, his existence had been little but work and accumulating wealth and possessions.

The master bedroom was downstairs. It would also be quite dark but he could go into his closet, shut the door, and dress by lighter flame.

A logical plan, he decided.

He started in that direction.

Halfway there, crossing a tiled foyer and stepping onto the soft hall carpet, he heard the unmistakable click of a gun as he passed the guest bathroom door.

Turning around at the sound, he felt the bullet sink into his groin simultaneously with a muted shot.

The killer grabbed the wounded man as he staggered, pushing him down on the floor, which had changed from expected soft carpet to the feel and smell of plastic sheeting against his naked skin.

A clothing bag for a costume...

The victim's brain automatically identified the improvised burial shroud as his palms pressed his belly, trying to block the traveling bullet fragments inside. Stretched on his back, his legs stiffened, deep unbearable pain pulsated into his abdomen.

He could not make a sound.

He stared into the eyes of his killer as the gun was leveled at his head.

Chapter 2

Marlotta Holt drummed her fingers on the fine marble-topped table where she beheld an untouched alcoholic drink.

The Men Unadorned Club was a cleverly designed private facility featuring talented young nude male gymnasts and dancers who entertained women over 30.

Unclothed members of the alpha sex, all tall and thin, danced with grace on a dimly lighted stage.

One step up.

Dual outreaching between performers and customers on the front row created a contact area.

Fingertips to skin only. Massage prohibited. No scratching allowed.

"Need some company?"

She studied the red haired naked man before her, automatically calculating length, scanning for height, estimating weight, counting freckles.

"You're new. Thanks but no thanks. I'm not interested."

It was not that the young male did not measure up.

Someone else was on her mind.

Marlotta rarely worried about her husband. However, tonight she was anxious.

She did not like this anxiety and she decided she was going to do something about it.

But she did not know what.

She was temporarily without transportation and dependent on the bus system so she could not look for him anywhere the bus would not travel.

She pulled her dumbphone out of her pocket.

The man's eyes popped.

"I hold a permit to carry. Mind your own business," she said with hostility.

"You look like Carlotta Fortune!"

Being compared to one of the most beautiful women who had ever lived, an iconic legend beyond her death, made Marlotta mad.

"I hate being told that. Don't mention that phony actress to me. I hope you don't use that line on other customers. I'll see you fired!"

Deflated, the man moved back to his pole and embraced it with devotion.

Marlotta punched the device.

It was dead.

She had not charged it.

Marlotta missed smartphones, outlawed by rigid dictates of the copyrightist movement, which had prevailed in forcing their entire agenda into law.

Landline phones now dominated.

She hated those phones and had refused to allow one to be wired in her house.

This refusal was dangerous, as there was no other way to call 911 emergency, but US citizens were within their rights to refuse a wired apparatus.

However, if they could get a license, individuals still had the option of paying for expensive cell service for a telephone that did nothing but facilitate limited messages and allow talking to others person to person, if both were on their devices.

If it was charged.

Marlotta's fist hit the table in frustration. She was too efficient to be so forgetful. It was an anomaly for her. Without her phone she had no other choice but to use what she considered the communication device of the lower classes.

She stood up, walked across the room, and got into a small glass booth, neglecting to shut its bifold door.

Imagine that I would stoop to this, she reflected grimly.

Marlotta Holt reached for the pay by coin telephone receiver to try to call her husband.

At least The Men Unadorned Club offered this convenience indoors. A luxury for those who could access the performance area. All females under 30 and all males of any age were restricted to the lobby or time travel sales office where landlines were private.

Most public facilities had pay by coin phones stationed out in the elements on sidewalks and street corners.

At the mercy of the weather, the antiquated devices brought back from the 20th century warehouses of non-computerized artifacts, needed constant maintenance and often did not work.

"You don't look old enough to be here," A slightly overweight blond nude young man approached her.

Marlotta laughed.

"To enter the performance area, you must possess documentation you are over 30 years old."

She wrinkled her nose. "That's a poor excuse for an overdone line. You can tell I am over 30 just by looking at my face. Just like I can tell you are over your weight limit."

He appeared to weigh nearly 165 while being only 6'2".

"I may not be able to deliver the lines well but I can deliver where it counts." He shifted his body.

"Off your diet? What is your name?"

"Loyce Smith. Just returned from vacation, mam. I'll be back in shape in no time." He pretended to exercise.

Marlotta's arm extended through the phone booth doorway. She playfully poked his slightly swollen stomach. "See that you are. Do you know who I am?"

"No mam. Just a beauty I spied from the stage. Though you do have a familiar look about you. Probably because I notice you out on the front row so often."

"Hmm. I have to use this contraption to make a phone call. To my husband. I also meet that entrance requirement. Now, shoo. Go back on stage and dance. I'll be watching."

The slightly overweight blond obeyed.

At least he has sense to follow the customer's wishes, Marlotta mentally acknowledged.

Pleased the dancer did not know she could fire him, Marlotta was enjoying the pretense she was a typical patron. And not too old yet to be still desirable to the younger men with whom she flirted.

A duplicity taking several forms.

Her legal age was 14 years younger than her biological age. Restrictions were severe for a successful application for an age change.

Age reduction petitioners to the courts had to look no older than their desired age and prove to judges they were in similarly youthful physical condition, unlikely to die younger than the current expected lifespan calculation for the age to which they aspired.

In addition, they had to prove they were not planning to commit fraud with their revised age. Plus they had to forgo any benefits accrued under their biological time clock for the number of years differed.

Marlotta had needed to reduce her age to marry.

She regretted it. The marriage trapped her. Her younger husband made so much money in his elite position.

And her work was private, yielding no prestige.

If she wished to retain her social status there could be no divorce.

A difficult daughter complicated the household.

So she haunted her establishment. Her husband did not comprehend that a need for mental release bound her to the club. He believed it was all business.

He never asked or bothered her about her work or any part of her life related to it.

Most of the time she was happy to be away from him. The time they spent together was cordial but too much togetherness and they would begin to bicker.

Most of the time she never gave him a thought when she was on her own.

Tonight she was lonely for him. It was a strange feeling but she decided to act on it.

No one answered the phone at her home.

"Excuse me, there is a message for you from the office." A short gray-brown haired woman in a chiffon skirt and silk blouse approached her, thrusting a written note inside the phone booth.

"Thanks, Amy."

Marlotta frowned at the paper.

"Who's this from?"

The employee stepped inside the booth and whispered into

Marlotta's ear. Marlotta stiffened. The other woman left hurriedly.

The pay by coin phone rang.

It could be Lars, hitting return call.

Marlotta was guessing.

The blond dancer approached her again, waving his body in a hula fashion.

"I suggest you get back to work," she barked at the young man. She waved him away, turning her back to him.

Looking somewhat offended, he wandered slightly away.

Torn between the note and the ringing payphone, she grabbed the receiver, put it to her ear, listening for several seconds.

The originator of the message and the caller turned out to be one and the same.

Marlotta shut the phone booth door.

"You crazy fool! Why did you also leave a message at the office! It didn't even say where you are. That was stupid. I'll be right there!" Her sharp angry words to the party on the other end of the line carried.

The nude male dancer had slipped off to the side of the room where shadows kept him opaque.

Unable to hear the conversation, he observed with interest as she slammed the phone receiver down, yanked the booth door open, crumpling the note and tossing it as she dashed out of the room, out of the building and into the night.

He nonchalantly strode towards the abandoned paper and swooped it up.

Note for Marlotta, 'Your phone dead. I need you here desperately at once,' it read.

"Oh well, one less headache tonight," he muttered, tightening his abdominal muscles as he headed back to the stage.

Chapter 3

The unclothed girl climbed the stairs in the dark, feeling each carpeted step with her bare feet.

An enchanting room where black and red moiré taffeta draperies shielded the window beckoned from the upper lancing.

The girl surveyed her lover's daughter's bedroom with curious jealousy.

A crystal lamp, promising illumination upon power restoration, still managed to reflect streetlight within the spacious area.

She could easily slip back into her shirt and pants.

Underwear was not a problem.

She never wore it.

She did not want to dress.

She tossed her clothes aside and stretched nude on the taffeta bedspread.

She wondered briefly if he would be willing to make love with her in the double bed.

No, he would have qualms about being with his mistress in his daughter's room.

She looked around, expecting to spot a stylish feminine landline phone suitable for a teenage girl.

Not familiar with landline technology, she desired to call him up to her.

However, there was no phone visible.

She deflated, recalling how her lover had complained his wife refused the utility, despite the safety implications.

Anger replaced curiosity.

The government's ban on smartphones in accordance with the strict copyright and trademark regulations was unfair and harmful to the public, newspapers screamed. The lack of revenue from monthly phone bills would bankrupt the phone companies triggering a national security risk.

Such protests happened in vain.

The government had just raised taxes and fees to subsidize the communications network.

A brisk black market in smartphones tempted the antisocial.

She wondered if any unlawful devices were secreted in the attractive furniture, if her lover's daughter was defiant.

She had left her own forbidden smartphone hidden in her grandparents' home, not daring to take the risk that she could be tracked to her lover's house.

She made a brief search of the bedroom but found nothing capable of communication.

Every item was politically correct save for one glaring contradiction.

She was astounded to discover a moiré taffeta 1860s style formal gown in the girl's dressing area.

Such garments were outlawed everywhere in the world as inflammatory, except in America where the Supreme Court had ruled the First Amendment barred clothing prohibitions.

Nevertheless, his daughter's possession of such a controversial piece would cause social ostracism and could get her father fired from his prominent sensitive position.

Accumulating cigarette lighters, no landlines in the house, French Dixie costumes in the closet, no wonder he says his family disregards his social position and puts him at risk of being fired, the girl reflected.

Overwhelmed by an outburst of love for the man she so desired, the girl decided to go back down and face her horror of the dark.

The electricity had not come back on. She decided it was not fair he should face that problem alone.

She was living and behaving as an adult.

It was time to act like one.

She feared the situation he endured was untenable.

Being caught with anyone under 21 in a sexual relationship was an executable offense for the adult and meant years of enforced psychiatric treatment for the underage participant.

The electricity failure was an unforeseen complication to a rendezvous that had been planned for weeks.

It could jeopardize everything.

His future and safety suddenly meant everything to her.

She was going to help him if she could.

She looked at the clock and saw more time had escaped than she felt. She questioned if she had dozed a little on the girl's bed.

She tossed her shirt and pants over her shoulder and trotted downstairs.

As her eyes adjusted to the dimmer scene, her last thought was a bewilderment as to why the foyer and hall were strewn with plastic garment bags.

She heard a small frightened whimper.

The last image her eyes beheld was the cat hiding behind a table.

A bullet permeated her brain freezing the feline's face in her mind as she fell.

Chapter 4

"I know what I saw. It was murder."

Debriah Brock had accepted this self-described witness as an emergency client.

"I was looking into the eyes of the second victim as she died."

Debriah was listening without commenting, avoiding eye contact.

"I admit I was trespassing."

Debriah nodded occasionally to facilitate continuance of narration.

"I was visiting a neighborhood home, looking for a place to stay inside. My person will not leave me alone in the house while she is at work. I love her but we are not enmeshed. She locks me out."

Counselor lingo, Debriah noted with some suspicion.

She nodded again.

"I lead a casual life. I don't impose limits on myself. I tend to wander and slip in anywhere there is an opening in the neighborhood vicinity. So I cannot actually tell you where I was. But I saw two people killed."

"What? People?"

Debriah lost her professional demeanor.

It was early morning. Another workday.

Now she was wide awake.

A 27-year-old professional single woman, Debriah Ann Brock worked at home, maintaining her office at the front of her house in a small room directly off her foyer, where she met with clients to counsel them.

Debriah lived in a suburban neighborhood right south of downtown Tyler, Texas where a city park bordered her on the north. It was the perfect location for a home office which quietly received clients one at a time.

"People! You mean dead people?"

The subject of Debriah's professional attention quieted at the sound of her voice, shrinking from her touch.

An early morning phone call yielded a little backstory that the client appeared to be in post-traumatic shock from some unknown incident.

Debriah had assumed the client was relating a natural act of aggression. She was prepared to successfully counsel victim and victor alike, plus witnesses and innocent bystanders.

Until the word 'people' dramatically altered the circumstances.

Self-satisfaction bolstered Debriah.

Most of her patrons presented problems with eating, sleeping, or twisted relationships with other felines.

This cat was confiding astounding events concerning people.

All those hours of studying cat relaxation techniques in graduate school, endless hours of listening to detailed dramas involving mice, birds, and snakes had paid off.

Now Debriah relished the chance to apply the fruits of these endeavors in a serious situation.

"I have to hear the details," Debriah insisted gently. "Please go on."

An audible sniff.

The story resumed.

"The girl appeared no older than 16. The man was married. I heard them talk about his wife. He was wearing a uniform of some kind. Before they undressed."

"A man in uniform and a teenage girl?"

"I did not know what to make of them. Or what to do."

"That's understandable. Now, are you sure it was not something on the television or the home shopping screen? You were in an unfamiliar environment."

"Of course. I am perfectly capable of telling the difference. The scents are entirely distinguishable."

"Right. I see."

Pushing back her long brown hair, which tended to fall the wrong way, Debriah now observed her counselee in detail.

She operated by letting clients relax before scrutinizing them overtly. That protocol prevented a lot of anxiety.

The witness's name was Carousel. She was a predominantly white calico with delicious markings of golden orange and black on her back and tail. Her face was almost all white but she had just enough color in her fur pattern to cause the top of her head and the edge of her forehead to produce a dramatic contrast to her eyes and nose.

Carousel posed primly in the patron basket with all four paws tucked under her.

She did not seem defensive or delusional. Her words were calm and underlined by a quiet purr.

"They were laughing and giggling. Talking, then they had apparently wonderful sex. After, they just hung out. They were so enjoying each other's company. Two humans in love. It was a joy to watch. My human is a solitary creature, depending on me and the canine for companionship."

"What happened to the two lovers?" Debriah wanted to keep Carousel's person out of the conversation.

So often cats became entangled in their emotional connection with their owner and would not discuss other human beings.

The species trait severely inhibited fact gathering.

But Carousel remained focused on her narrative.

"Then the lights went out. Naturally, I could still see. But heavy moiré taffeta curtains prevented the humans from seeing properly. And it was a cloudy dusk. The man planned to get the lights back on by flipping the breakers. But-."

Carousel stretched out and hid her face inside the crook of one leg.

Purring stopped.

"I know it must be traumatic for you. But you need to tell me everything you remember."

Carousel pulled herself back up with dignity. She flipped her luscious tail around her paws, hiding retracted claws. She had extremely sharp claws and had to be very careful not to injure humans accidentally when they picked her up.

"Meow," she said, blinking hard.

Debriah could feel the lines of communication growing thin.

"Concentrate on me," she told Carousel. "Tell it to me just like you would tell a fictional story. Try not to let any emotions creep in."

Carousel gazed thoughtfully at her counselor. She was a strong-minded cat, quite able to follow those instructions.

Still it had been a harrowing experience.

Her person had no idea how to react when the feline had returned home dazed and in shock.

Carousel needed assistance processing such incomprehensible human activity.

She had previously noticed Debriah Brock's prominent phone book ad, which bore enough fruit to generate moderate income for the cat whisperer.

The directory perpetually on the telephone table, it had been an easy paw maneuver to flip it open and find the right page.

The owner responded as if it contained a message meant only for her. She rushed Carousel to the counselor.

A dire diagnosis on the spot resulted in temporarily relinquished custody.

The cat was staying with Debriah for the foreseeable future until she was no longer in danger of withdrawing into a catatonic state.

Now in the first stages of interaction, Debriah summoned all her skills. First she endeavored to gain Carousel's trust.

She ceased talking and got down on her knees to be eye level with the cat.

Began cautiously scratching Carousel on the top of the head.

Then under the chin.

Carousel stood and stretched.

Then Debriah applied a stronger massage going down the spine and scratching just below the tail.

Carousel maneuvered to one side, exited the counselee basket and crawled into Debriah's lap.

Finally the feline reclined her ears and a faint purr ensued.

Debriah reintroduced a soothing tone into the process.

After a nose kiss, the cat resumed her place in the basket and indicated she was ready to talk again.

"You don't have to begin at the beginning. Just tell me what you feel comfortable sharing."

The calico began with the aftereffects, which were still inducing some post-traumatic stress in her mind.

"I was so stressed I had double vision and my scent discernment failed in confusion. I had to clean myself for three days before I got off all the blood off my fur…"

Chapter 5

The police detective had granted an emergency interview. Routine dictated ordinary citizens had to progress through a long line of clerks and patrol officers before reaching the highest-ranking official on the premises.

The elderly couple had cited their ages in their petition.

Dreading unnecessary Death Options or ageism accusations, and the ensuing avalanche of paperwork, the captain welcomed them into his office, a small gray windowless square with a desk full of papers, an office chair, a monotonous clip fan, and a large corner fireplace.

Uniformed personnel brought in two chairs from other offices to face the captain's workspace.

In the chair on the right, the woman got straight to the point.

"Our granddaughter is missing. She's only 16. Please help us."

"You have no contact with her?"

"Ever since she had to turn in her phone, it has been so hard to keep tabs on her. She is independent. She refused a GPS implant."

Captain Raize Parks stifled a flash of anger at the ban of smartphones.

Those behind the regulations ostensibly wanted all means of copying images, downloading broadcasts, and otherwise procuring any form of entertainment destroyed.

After the laws had been rolled out slowly over a number of years, the last personal devices capable of such action had been confiscated over two years ago.

Raize Parks saw the movement as an attempt to hamper law enforcement activities.

The statutes made tracking deviceless people almost impossible unless they consented to a GPS implant.

The public was not told that many criminals kept their smartphones in defiance.

So did a lot of rebellious teenagers.

However, the missing girl, Magdalene Rene Watters, had turned hers in.

"Were you or your granddaughter involved in the protest movement?"

It came to Raize's mind that the girl may be a victim of delayed retaliation by the copyrightist movement. Though victorious, they had not forgotten their opponents and were still pursing them in and out of court.

If the complainants had been vocal enough to provoke an extremist group, the disappearance of a descendant could be a direct result of their political dissent.

Robbing people of the chance to ensure their lineage continued constituted a common form of terrorism.

The Watters couple, both graying thin individuals, appeared obviously not unaware of this possibility.

"Our granddaughter respects the law. We raised Magdalene Rene from an infant. She is the only child of our only daughter." The man in the left chair spoke loudly.

"Don't shout, dear. This officer seeks to help us. Please understand, Captain, we love her very much."

Raize observed a softness to Mrs. Watters which echoed her calm manner, belied only by twisting her hands repeatedly.

"And Magdalene Rene's parents? Are they in the picture?"

"No." The elderly man's voice remained terse but his volume dropped.

Mr. Watters presented an abrupt contrast to his wife. His tall angled body wracked with twisted tension as he glared.

"Her father is in prison, convicted in 2099."

Raize nodded respectfully. "Convicted for his political views? For opposing the copyrightists?"

"For trafficking in undocumented depression glass. And selling prohibited foods on the side. He isn't political."

"He was arrested before she was born and still has 12 years on his sentence for the glassware offense. He had not been tried for selling ice cream. He could spend the rest of his life in prison."

"They never married." The grandfather frowned his disapproval.

"And your daughter?"

"Magdalene Rene's mother was born to us late in our lives. We had to apply for approval to rear her since we were over the age limit to have children."

Raize studied the couple intently.

It was impossible to discern their ages.

He decided they probably had obtained legally reduced ages anyway, making their biological ages confidential. Their listed first names, Earl and Earlene, indicated they were no stranger to status change petitions.

"But you obtained approval?"

"Yes." Mrs. Watters dabbed her eyes with a tissue. "The great joy of our lives. Unfortunately our daughter took a Death Option as a result of her profession."

"Damn Death Options. It's people with jobs like yours that made them so popular with regular people."

Mr. Watters was coming close to illegal insubordination but Raize let it pass.

He had respect for those left from the bygone eras with enough courage and cleverness to survive, not understanding the contemporary attraction of a Death Option now that life after death was a certainty.

Sometimes resistance pays off, he reflected.

A long earthly life was not an anathema to the detective.

"All this technology and there is not any way to find her?"

"Not unless she had allowed for the traceable implant chip."

Mrs. Watters cried for few seconds.

"What profession did your daughter practice that had a Death Option? And how long ago?"

"Veterinary technician. She was in charge of feeding a panther and died due to the animal refusing domestication in 2100."

"I'm sorry for your loss."

Too long ago to be relevant, thought Raize.

"She did receive a posthumous certificate of merit from her employer and her picture is on the wall at the animal refugee center along with others who sacrificed their lives for the wildlife."

"We are most proud of that." The man's tone did not resonate the conviction of pride. "The panther got away with it. Entrapment, they said."

"Never mind about lessons learned decades ago. What about our granddaughter? She is all we have left." Mrs. Watters was still sniffling.

"Is there any way the FBI can be called in?"

"Not at this stage, regrettably."

The FBI, one of the few governmental agencies with computer file access, investigated a limited range of crimes.

Those included collection and copyright violations, mismatched age relationships, conflicting beliefs, smoking, ice cream sales, illegal devices, misuse of 3D printers, unlawful object modification, and a few obscure similar crimes.

The FBI only investigated murder if there was a mass shooting, political assassination, or a misuse of the Death Option. They only investigated the lost after 180 days and only if the absentee was under 40.

Local police had to take care of everything else.

Raize Roberts Parks became a police officer when he was 30 years old. Now senior man stationed at his department, since police chiefs worked from home, he had seen many changes in almost 20 years.

Yet the solving of crimes containing elements of mystery still was the domain of the elite few with the innate talent of scoping out the truth when confronted with webs of deceit.

Raize Parks was one of those people

Raize had a rare gift of solving crimes that defied conventional analysis.

He needed the FBI only because he needed their technology. Getting assistance was not easy but he knew of a few loopholes. He had to be circumspect in fishing through them.

The Watters were little aware of how blessed they were to report to him personally and his next question gave them little insight into this good fortune.

"Is she a registered collector?" He pursued alternative angles.

"No, like most, we are registered gun collectors so we can

26

carry pistols. But she had not registered yet."

"But, I mean, is she registered to collect anything? Dolls? Fake fingernails? Bears? Christmas tree ornaments."

"No."

"And are you sure she had no illicit pastimes? Video gaming?"

"NO."

"We know that activity is the main unlawful sport of students. It does rate FBI investigation due to device regulations."

"As an animal lover, taking after her mother, she respected the Supreme Court's decision to outlaw video gaming after scientists demonstrated gaming addictions contributed to a significant increase in pet suicide."

"She had also applied for a grant to study the animosity between some cats and dogs."

"Has Magdalene Rene any conflicting beliefs that could be documented?"

"No."

"And her relationships? All with guys her own age?"

"She had no forbidden relationships with romance or sex attached."

There was one other possibility.

"And, I have to ask, any terrorism sympathies. Particularly French Dixie tendencies?"

French Dixie terrorism posed a here and now ominous menace, which had claimed thousands of lives around the world since its origins as simple fashion fad in France had led to a bloody civil war in France almost 30 years ago.

Mrs. Watters protested the idea that her granddaughter had French Dixie sympathies.

"Absolutely not!"

"No, no way. She wears only ordinary clothing."

Designers had kicked off the cultural battle as a fashion trend a decade before the actual conflict. Women wearing hoop skirts and men in gray trousers and tunics dominated the news media and entertainment industry proclaiming a new French order. The movement had slowly overtaken French society until it evolved into a political force dictating all women had to dress in 1800s styles and gradually introducing laws from that era.

Raize had exhausted the list of activities in which the girl might be involved making her important enough for him to handle it personally, much less involve the FBI.

He did not want to be forced to hand the case off to a patrol officer. He could broach Electra surreptitiously about this problem.

The detective opened his phone to Electra Simpson's stored number. His phone, being the highest grade license, permitted an unlimited number of calls and texts, still counting against recipients' allotments.

Electra had a smartphone. Only government officials such as the FBI had such devices. There was not only no limit on their calls but also no records maintained.

As if they were never made.

In addition, Electra could connect to the Internet.

If that alone did not make her invaluable, she had shared, somewhat laughingly, somewhat embarrassed that computerized methods had paired them in an old fashioned illegal dating software program.

Statues with concrete specifications now governed legal relationships.

She was his only friend in the FBI and their relationship, while ethical due to a dual clandestine investigation, was still developing.

As he courteously and consolingly dismissed the worried grandparents, a pressure arose in his throat.

Interacting with Electra Simpson had evolved into a self-improving chore which he both dreaded and anticipated with relief simultaneously.

An action needed, required to move forward…

She was his computer designated mate.

Procrastination thwarted, he reached for the phone.

Required to grow old…

Chapter 6

"Can I help?" asked Samantha. "What is up?"

"My latest client thinks she witnessed two murders. Only there is no report anything happened." Debriah shifted with exasperation.

"Sounds like a nut case. You have to keep in mind the species you are dealing with. They can be unreliable. How is it going otherwise? Professionally, I mean." Samantha Speer stretched out on her coffin style sofa, with detachable lid. She enjoyed lounging on it whenever she was not working. She pulled the lid partway down.

In order to make eye contact with her friend, Debriah had to perch on the edge of Samantha's professional office chair.

Samantha lived and worked in a home similar to Debriah's house. She dwelt just down the street.

"Where is this drama queen?"

"She's not. You are prejudging her. Don't be so specist. She's very sweet and shy. In fact, she needed some alone time, so I had to get out of the house."

"Sweet and shy? A cat? Your business is getting to you. You need a break."

"You cannot say there's never any demand for cat whisperers. I'm booked solid until Christmas."

"That good?" Samantha looked a little jealous. No court-ordered vampire counseling had come her way recently. Walk-ins were rare.

Debriah could not help but brag a little.

"Christmas is so profitable. People who ignore their pets all year suddenly crave to know how to please them during the holidays. Either out of a Christian spirit or just to make them behave for guests and during parties. But the rest of the year runs slow."

"I still think it was a mistake for you to take a position as a cat whisperer when you could make much more money as a psychic."

"I don't like psychic work."

"I wish I had more than one career certification so I could do more than just vampire consolation," said Samantha. "People are always unhappy with the results, whichever way it goes."

"Turn your hobby into a second career," suggested Debriah.

"I may have to. The movement to legalize vampirism is growing. But it still has a long way to go. If I do become a painter, I'll be able to retire and draw Artistic Impact Security by then."

"You will have a hard time getting certified with landscapes since taking photos of landscapes is still legal, unlike photographing people. You just have to get a camera permit."

"Didn't you hear? They've changed the law again. People with permitted cameras had to turn them in last week."

"No, I didn't know." Debriah's eyebrows rose.

"Yes, just like smartphones. Legal now only for government officials, and not many of them. No more photography at all."

Debriah dismissed her initial stressful dismay. "I don't have a camera anyway. I'd rather capture likenesses by hand."

"You have so many more options than me. If I could capture facial likenesses I would never deal with vampires. You could junk this cat whisperer job and devote your time to your portraits."

"That sounds fine in theory. But artistic certifications do not come with health insurance. And, having been diagnosed with Time Travel Imbalance, I'm uninsurable."

"I wish I had Time Travel Imbalance. It must be wonderful, like getting to travel in time for free. Just recently, I saw a Jack the Ripper Time Travel Experience for $5,000 a night."

"It is not wonderful! I fall back in time abruptly and have no control over what happens. It's a disease."

Time Travel Imbalance did not carry as much of a stigma as most diseases that affected the distribution of matter in time and space but Debriah had been misdiagnosed with the more ostracized ailments before it had been discovered exactly what she had.

Those days still haunted her.

Samantha was familiar with Debriah's history but, as all those not afflicted with any major illness, did not completely understand.

There was a short awkward silent.

"Look at us. Two single eligible attractive women just sitting around evaluating our lives. What I do believe is there are a lot of people having a lot more fun than us tonight," Samantha declared.

"I don't know if I want to go out. If what Carousel relates is true, there is a killer in the area. Her person's house is in this neighborhood and the cat probably did not wander too far away."

"So the bodies should be found in house near our places?"

"Correct."

"There is one safe place we could go. The library."

"The library?"

"Yes. Rent a bed for reading. They created new special effect locations. Space travel. Ancient Egypt. *Titanic*. All done with props supplementing the books."

"Library? You want to go to the library?"

"I recently volunteered to serve on the Campaign to Reinvigorate Libraries."

Samantha groaned. "How did you get roped into that?"

"Oh, I just get tired of saying no to all these campaigns and this one seemed like it would be no trouble. Since relocating adjacent to hospitals, public libraries have introduced private bed rental sections behind curtains for a small fee."

"Hospital beds for entertainment?"

"Of course not. These beds are in the center of the library, surrounded by the book stacks. Romantic daybeds behind rounded curtains. Most spaces are economy with only a book and a cup of cocoa. But if you want to spend more money, they have several diverse bedtime experiences to choose from, located in the basement."

"Have you actually done this?"

"Well, no. All I have to do is refer two people a month for one year to fill my quota. I get a community service certificate."

"Excellent sales pitch but the library just won't do."

"What do you suggest?"

"The Men Unadorned Club."

"An over-30 ladies club. How will we get in? They promote time travel on the side. That's not why you want me to go there?"

"Of course not. The floorshow is the only entertainment I can afford. Exquisite male performers. And I'll get us in."

"I might could find some good looking men to paint," said Debriah. "Are they really nude?"

31

"Naturally. And there is a contact zone."

"Hmm, well, I am between men right now. But I don't want any time travel sale pitch, understand?"

"Perfectly. That is in a separate section of the building. We'll steer clear. No vacations. Just naked men for us tonight."

Chapter 7

"This is our guide to safe fun and perfect leisure. An authentic Jack the Ripper Time Travel Experience."

A woman handed a brochure to the elderly couple. The time travel advertisement was colorful but vague, promising only a short excursion to one of several settings.

"As you see, lessor trips are also available at lower costs."

The trip the couple sought was not on the list.

"You offer a French Dixie experience?" the man asked.

"Where did you get that idea? That would be against the law, of course."

The couple glanced at each other.

"We hear it from one of our friends who recommended your, um, service."

"Pardon me, madam. I have to speak with someone in the hall."

The woman left the couple alone in the small office strategically dominated by a large china cabinet with dense stained glass windows. The small desk and chair in one corner and the compact sofa across from it shrank in comparison.

Mrs. Watters had seen a young man proceed through a different door marked closet and had to be restrained from following him.

"Earlene, I do regard this as dangerous. Especially at our ages. Here we are in some inner sanctum that is only accessible through their office complex. This cannot be prudent behavior on our part."

"Earl, I can do this alone if necessary. You don't have to come. But it is critical that we explore every possibility of tracking our granddaughter. All we have to go on is this number in that illegal smartphone we found in her room. It was the only number that could not be explained. We dialed it and it has led us here."

"You don't fathom that she took one of the time travel trips and got lost in the past."

"No, of course not. But, my dear, something must have caused

33

her to highlight this phone number in her list of contacts with the notation 'French Dixie, Marlotta' beside it. And it appears to be the only number she ever dialed from that forbidden phone. What a risk she took in calling such a place. And I don't believe for a second she was sneaking in here to watch these men dance. She looked far too young to get in."

"I agree we have got to know what happened and why and how she got that number. But shouldn't we have just turned it over to Captain Parks?"

"I don't want to do that. When Magdalene Rene is found, I don't want her to immediately be in trouble with the law."

"True."

The woman abruptly returned. She gave them a false smile.

"Mr. and Mrs. Watters, I am confident that for an extra fee we can accommodate you in a French Dixie time travel adventure of a lifetime."

"Indeed?"

"Wonderful!" Mrs. Watters cleared her throat. "I understand you are the manager."

"Yes, I am."

"Do you employ a guide named Marlotta by any chance? That was the name recommended to me."

Alarm crossed the other woman's face.

No more smiles.

"You must be mistaken. The name connected with the French Dixie movement most often is Carlotta, you recall the actress Carlotta Fortune?"

"Of course."

"That must have been the name you heard. She is, uh, dead but sometimes is, um, available in our journeys to the past."

This assertion caused Mr. Watters to tense. Mrs. Watters took a deep breath.

"You do comprehend that at your ages, time travel could be dangerous. There is some element of physiology involved that could be detrimental to your health. You must take an opiate prior to commencement. You might want to think it over."

"You mentioned more money. How much more?"

The woman hesitated, then wrote a figure on a brochure and handed it to the couple, then perched on the desk, folding her arms.

Silently the two elderly people passed it back and forth, both having to absorb it slowly.

A multiple 10 times the original price quoted.

"Let us think it over," said Mr. Watters.

"Of course, I understand. If time travel is beyond your budget, I hear the library is offering imaginative environments."

Everyone stood up.

"May I use your restroom?"

"Certainly, Mr. Watters. Just go back out into our outer offices. Mrs. Watters, would you care to wait inside the performance area?"

"Oh, my, thank you, yes."

The elderly couple exited the small inner office, parted, and went in opposite directions.

Mrs. Watters slipped into the performance area of The Men Unadorned Club and took a seat.

Chapter 8

A completely shaven male performed directly in front of Debriah and Samantha as they sipped chocolate shakes disguised as alcoholic drinks.

"I feel so much stress over this client, I am beside myself. I must concentrate on my main problem in the here and now."

"Wonder if he uses a razor or a cream?" Samantha smiled encouragingly at the dancer.

"I don't know. But this illicit shake does not taste like genuine ice cream. I suspect it is fake."

"If it were real ice cream the police would shut this place down. Did you call them about the cat?"

"I explained to the police but they say Carousel must be hallucinating. They requested her name but I don't dare reveal her identity. They might put her in a feline counseling sanitarium if no evidence of a murder emerges. Cats are so discriminated against. No one believes them unless there is evidence they are telling the truth."

"That's because they are cats."

Catching the word 'cats' the entertainer began imitating a feline on stage.

"It's not fair. Everyone believes horses and dogs when they report a crime through their counselors. And there are many dogs and even a few horses who lie."

"You ladies into animals?" The hairless man broke his routine and pulled up a chair.

"Absolutely not!" Samantha exclaimed.

"I just talk to cats," said Debriah calmly.

The man backed away, leaving the chair empty.

"Cat talker?"

"I'm a cat whisperer," said Debriah.

"I'm a vampire counselor, an officer of the court." Samantha drummed her fingers on the table.

No tip here.

"Oh, I see. Well, I'm due for my break anyway. Nice to have met you."

He retreated towards the restrooms.

"I think he misinterpreted your explanation."

"Saves trouble sometimes. I will report him for animal abuse if I get even a hint he is into that."

A man with a sharply trimmed auburn beard and other hair to match circled the table.

Samantha slipped him a bill.

"Very nice. Thank you."

"I didn't think he danced that well."

"I was not tipping his dancing. Does the household Carousel belongs to include a dog also? Or a horse perhaps? Who are her owners?"

"She just has one person. A woman named Amy Raxel. She appears to be a devoted pet owner. But does not leave her animals in the house when she is at work."

"Isn't that negligence?"

"Some animals do need to roam. And the Supreme Court did rule that was not unconstitutional."

"Do you have access to her other pets?"

"There is a dog but he is not involved. I do grasp what you're getting at. You think I should do a little investigating of my own?"

"I don't see why not."

"Say, doesn't that woman over there look familiar?"

"The old lady staring at the stage with her mouth open?"

"No, that one." Debriah pointed to a middle-aged woman.

"You know, she does look familiar to me. But probably because I've seen her here frequently."

"But I've never been here. I've seen her somewhere else."

A four-man mariachi band, wearing only large colorful hats began making its way around the tables.

Samantha motioned them over.

"Why did you do that?"

The music became loud and Debriah protected her ears. After a song, Samantha tipped them and waved them away.

"These men in here are always twisting and turning. I wanted to compare those four standing side by side."

"Why?"

"Just latent professional curiosity. I did my psychology practicum working as a male measurement specialist for the army, remember?"

"And that job convinced you to choose another field, I recall."

"Oh, yes. When those men did not pass, I had to use my skills to keep them from suicide sometimes. That's why I switched to Vampire Consolation. Vampires are almost never suicidal. Now it's gotten worse since military Death Options have been extended to war games. So many Death Options exercised just to make war games more realistic."

"I know. It's the times. Just like years ago they did not always kill the actors and actresses who accept the roles of murder victims like they do now." Samantha waved at a blond dancer watching her and ordered another drink, legal liquor this time.

"I hear the actors unions are going to start protesting that."

"I should think so. You know it all started with Carlotta Fortune taking her Death Option in that movie, *Twilight of the French South*. She was so marvelous, the film was unforgettable."

"Alive and ignored or dead and acclaimed? What's it to be? You know, I don't recall I've ever seen that show. Just heard it talked about ad nauseam. How did you ever get to see it?"

"There was a court ordered showing just two years ago under civil immunity because of a legal technicality in the Freedom of Communications Act. Don't you remember?"

"I vaguely recollect a lot of carrying on about that."

"Just as the government feared, it revived the French Dixie movement, as if it had ever faded."

"I wish that blond dancer would move closer. I can't see enough."

"Carlotta Fortune landed the lead female role in the defining fictional statement about the French Dixie war. A self-sacrificial taking of her Death Option at the end of the story capped a great performance. At least 13 famous actresses have taken Death Options at the age of 36 just to emulate her. Who knows how many unknowns did the same? My mother told me stories about all that when I was younger."

"You should get back on friendly terms with your parents." Samantha stood up. "I still cannot see him clearly."

"Carlotta Fortune has a cult following of millions. She really made taking the Death Option acceptable for people in nonviolent occupations. Don't you know any Hollywood history?"

"Hollywood history classes were not required for my major. Oh, damn, he went the other way."

"It was all above board then. I hear sometimes it is not disclosed all the roles which contain Death Options. They hire the performers without giving them the full script."

"That should definitely be against the law." Samantha sighed deeply.

Debriah took that to mean she cared about the conversation.

"Since science has proven there is life after death, people's attitudes changed. Actors crave fame. They don't realize canceled shows are forgotten when the next hit comes along."

"And death may not be the end but it is still final." Samantha was feeling a little giddy. She plopped back down in her chair.

"That's why that woman over there looks familiar. She looks like Carlotta Fortune. Only older than Carlotta lived to be."

Samantha stared but her vision was no longer sharp.

"No, I don't think so. Look, the mariachi band is surrounding that elderly woman. She's getting up. She's, she's dancing!"

Samantha took a gulp.

Debriah placed a firm hand on her arm.

"I need to dance!"

"Absolutely not," Debriah said.

"Oh, the old lady's leaving. I wonder why?"

"Probably had something to do with the old man who is yelling at her from the lobby."

"I suppose so," said Samantha. "I don't know why she would go with him instead of the band."

Chapter 9

"I wish we had just gone ahead and paid all the money."

Simultaneously consumed with regret while feeling invigorated, Mrs. Watters was driving home.

They would never get another chance to try to find Magdalene Rene by investigating time travel at The Men Unadorned Club.

They had already attracted too much attention. Concluding hard-core French Dixie terrorists were involved, Mrs. Watters feared she and Mr. Watters might vanish like Magdalene Rene.

And I'll probably never get to go back and see the whole show, she thought sadly, then smiled. *But what I did get to see!*

"We don't possess that much money! And to put it on a credit card would tie up our finances for years."

"I expect the price went up because we mentioned the name Marlotta." Mrs. Watters sighed sadly.

"We should have waited until we got the price, then asked questions."

"I know it. I am kicking myself as I am driving this car. Hard to do strapped in as I am." Her quip provoked her husband to smile.

The Watters owned a luxury Pacifica. The automobile could drive itself except Mrs. Watters preferred to keep control.

Earl Watters wondered that the lift in his wife's voice belied her distress at their failure at the club. His smile was fleeting. "Maybe Magdalene Rene did get it wrong. Likely she misspelled the name."

"You remember I was a big fan of that old TV show the Fortune sisters starred in?"

"You watched it incessantly."

"That woman reminded me of Darlotta, the triplet who wasn't identical. Only this person was much older, yet not as old as Darlotta would be now."

"Probably hired because of the resemblance."

"Yes, but Darlotta Fortune quit acting when she became of age. She had nothing to do with the movie. Still there was another woman in the audience I noticed resembled the Fortune girls, only likewise much older."

"Lookalikes, employed to foster the atmosphere of nostalgia."

"Their heyday ended decades ago."

"This business is pushing time travel."

"And should it be more than nostalgia, more than reenacting French Dixie culture, should this facility engage in real terrorism-Earl, I fear we will never see Magdalene Rene again."

Earl Watters agreed. "I bet they got her."

"I wish we could have gathered evidence to report to that police captain, but we failed."

"Did you spy anything when you went inside the club? They wouldn't let me in the performance area. The music blared so loud, even in the lobby, I had to yell at the top of my voice to get your attention."

Mrs. Watters cleared her throat, recalling her short rest at a table inside the women-only performance area while Mr. Watters spent some time in the restroom.

A long time in the restroom.

Distress over Magdalene Rene's suspected plight faded at the recollection.

Earlene Watters had seen quite a lot.

"Nothing memorable." She flushed. She had rarely fibbed to her husband of more than half a century.

"Waste of time then?"

I'll never forget that Mariachi band as long as I live, she thought, all guilt evaporating. *It was worth it…*

"No -oh, I wouldn't say that, Earl. I, uh, was able to see the bigger picture. You know something good comes out of every experience."

"Hmm. That's your attitude. I think we wasted our time."

Mrs. Watters did not reply.

She was recalling every detail of the anatomy of the young tall thin red haired man with sharp facial hair who had paid her particular attention.

The red headed gymnast with the pointed beard slipped off the stage to present me a rose and kiss my hand, she remembered dreamily.

"Watch where you're going!"

Mrs. Watters had to swerve sharply to avoid a collision with an oncoming vehicle.

"Earlene! Do you need me to drive? You know at our ages if we are injured in an automobile wreck the insurance companies will want to total us!"

"Calm down, dear. A miss is as good as a mile." Mrs. Watters strove to keep her voice calm.

"The pressure to take our age related Death Options will be severe."

"But we still don't have to take Death Options if we don't feel ready. The law says we have the right to refuse, no matter what the insurance companies say."

"No telling how much longer that will be," grumbled Mr. Watters.

He settled back down as his wife slowed the car and drove more steadily.

Now where was I? Oh, yes, that young man had such... Such…. Vitality… Yet the clean-shaven man was so unique. If I had to choose, it would be impossible…

"Earl?"

"Yes, dear?"

"I hope you are not too tired after all this… You are not going to want to go right to sleep?"

And his wife gave him a glance that from many years of married life, he knew meant he was not going to get any rest at all this night…

42

Chapter 10

Having retrieved her car from the shop, now back at The Men Unadorned club, Marlotta Holt nibbled at her salad and sampled the floorshow.

Business took her mind off personal troubles.

Those two girls at that table over there don't look over 30.

She eyed the younger women, one a dark haired beauty, the other with coal black hair but a more complicated facial structure.

An attractive blond dancer moved closer to her table and Marlotta forgot the other women.

Marlotta's eyebrows rose.

This was the same man she recalled snooping about when she used the payphone.

She shook off images of her husband. She had been on cordial terms with him so she had envisioned.

Now she felt he had rejected her with finality.

Despite her basic low emotion personality, Marlotta did have feelings.

Her husband's abdication of his spousal role still hurt.

At least I still have some family left, she mused. *And these beguiling men...need more of them...*

The young nude man was glancing her way.

She took another drink and tried to concentrate on him. Any relationship with him would be highly risky...

I don't need to make a move yet, she thought, as he swung nearer. *I can get at him anytime...*

"Papers, ladies."

A clothed employee of the club approached Samantha and Debriah's table.

Samantha somewhat unsteadily handed over two folders from her purse.

The employee looked at both women, nodded, returned the documentation and moved on.

"How did you ever get these false documentations saying we were over 30?" Debriah asked in a whisper.

She and Samantha enjoyed eyeing the same nude blond as Marlotta but from another side of the room.

"On the Internet." Samantha took a sip of her liquor as she sotto-voiced a reply.

"My God!" Debriah's voice rang out so that several patrons at nearby tables looked in her direction despite the loud music.

The blond man angled over towards their location.

"Shhh!" Samantha shook a slightly inebriated finger, her eyes on the man.

"You're going to wind up in jail! You surf? You know you're going to get caught."

"You are so naïve. The Internet is still legal in South America. All you have to do is get a directed connection. No one can catch me here."

"Oh, Samantha. You don't realize there are no secrets anymore. Everyone knows everything."

"You've been talking to too many cats. Hey, look at that red headed guy with the long long… looong…"

"Yes, I see him," Debriah said impatiently.

Samantha's revelation of illegally accessing the Internet had ruined her enjoyment of the club's offerings. Their fraudulent papers, if not used for fraud, would mean nothing more than a fine if they were caught.

In addition, it could be argued that the paperwork represented art or constituted research for a fiction book, so a penalty might not even be levied.

But accessing the Internet could mean prison.

"Looong hair," Samantha continued, her words becoming more slurred.

"Strange, I didn't see that person check the ID of the woman who looks like an older Carlotta Fortune." Debriah stood up.

Samantha rose also. "That's cause she looks old enough to be here. Sit down until I get back. I have to use the restroom."

Debriah dropped into her chair and watched Samantha take off.

Samantha rounded a corner, out of Debriah's sight.

But no other customers seem to be escaping the document check, Debriah observed.

In a darkened corridor leading to the restrooms, Samantha paused to catch her breath when she felt a hand on her shoulder.

"I could not help seeing you at the table with your companion." The blond man gripped her arms, holding her firmly in place. "I'm Loyce. I hoped to meet you before you left and extend a personal invitation to you to come back. With or without your friend."

"I, um, will come back."

"Promise?" He turned them both. She was in the dark but light from the outer area fell on him.

Samantha swayed. Loyce's bright blue eyes danced in front of her. She dropped her eyes and her gaze landed on his exterior.

Had she been sober, she never would have reached.

She was far from sober.

And surrounded by golden hair, it looked so beautiful.

"Um."

He picked her up as she grabbed him.

"Let's go in here."

And in a second he had her through door labeled closet, closing it behind her, undressing her as he guided down a dark hall and into a small windowless room.

A rather coarse material rubbed her skin and realized she was down on a small bed with rough cotton sheets.

"You enjoy sex?" He pulled the rest of her clothes off.

"I'm- um-, normally-"

He interrupted her comments by placing his mouth over hers and his hand over her interior.

"Ready? You are ready."

Before she could reply or agree, he was inside.

She passed out.

"Did you faint from the intensity or the booze?"

He was calmly covering her when she awoke.

"I, uh, what did you do? Who are you?"

"It was love at first sight. Finish dressing. I've got to get back to work. What's your name?"

"Samantha Speer."

"I want to marry you. You're not married, are you?"

"No. I. Hey?"

"Thank goodness. Me neither. How old are you? I'll bet you are not over 30 either. I bet you aren't." He opened her purse. "I'll just take one of your cards. Oh, you're a vampire consultant?"

Samantha, sobered abruptly from the experience, stood up with some hostility.

"I'm almost 30. Do you have a vampire problem?" She grabbed her purse and raised it threateningly.

He held up his hands defensively. "No way. Absolutely not. I'm a libertarian."

"A libertarian? I could get you for rape! If you say you are a vampire, I'm going to prosecute."

"Now you know if a woman is intoxicated a man cannot be charged with rape. That law was passed when we were children. Besides I am most emphatically not saying I'm a vampire. I loathe vampirism and I never have had that problem."

Samantha stared at him.

His eyes glowed, large and calm and blue.

Her mind drifted…

"We are the same age, aren't we?"

"Just about, I imagine. I'm 28." He closed her purse and handed it to her.

"Oh, I'm 27!"

"No conflicts, I'm sure of it. We can get married anytime. I'm sure it will be approved. You planning on children?"

"Yes. I do. I, uh, never dreamed this would happen to me. What's your name?"

"Loyce, um, Loyce Smith."

"I- I don't know what to say."

"Just consider it. Listen, don't say anything to your friend. Or anybody. Just keep quiet. I'll get in touch soon."

"Okay. Uh, do you live here?"

Loyce hesitated.

"They do provide us quarters to sleep in if we want. I'm here most of the time. But don't come here looking for me. I'll get in touch with you."

"Okay. I guess."

"All I ask is a fair consideration."

"I'm sorry I passed out. But, yes, maybe. Maybe."

"Good." He kissed her gently and left.

Getting her bearings, Samantha exited into the dark hall.

Spotting her original destination, she slipped into the restroom.

She nodded to several women there who seemed not to notice anything different about her.

After, she cautiously crept back out into the performance area.

Loyce emerged, performing as though nothing had occurred. He did not glance at her.

Before Samantha returned to the table, Debriah found her and pointed her towards the exit.

"I've paid the bill already," said Debriah.

Samantha remembered she had been intoxicated at the time she had left Debriah.

She decided to obey Loyce and keep the encounter a secret.

It would be hard to explain that she had fallen in love, had sex, and was now planning marriage and children, all from a trip to the restroom.

She managed to act drunk.

"Are we leaving? No-ooooh! See the red headed guy? He's leaving the stage! I never got to meet him!"

"I'm taking you home. You are inebriated. I do have some responsibility to you. You are my only friend."

"I was just trying to get us some relaxation."

As Debriah dragged Samantha towards the doorway, firmly steering her out of the building, Marlotta noticed them once again.

Marlotta regretted her impulsive marriage deeply.

Why did I complicate my life?

A shift in the music caused her to turn her attention back towards the stage.

Regrettably, the young blond man left.

Marlotta resolutely banished the younger women from her mind as her eyes searched the males performing, hoping to glimpse another as pleasing as the absent blond dancer.

She settled on the completely shaven dancer.

She approached the stage and got his attention.

"Want to make some extra money?"

"Sure."

"Then listen closely. I have to pick up someone so I won't be around for a while. You have to pay attention the first time."

"I have excellent retention."

"Fine. I am one of those in charge here and I want you for a role-play. Now it's a chance for you to move up in the organization and increase your pay considerably."

"Wonderful. Anything you want."

"Come with me and I'll show you what to do."

Chapter 11

After the rugged routine of Army life, Bonita prepared to spend time among the moiré taffeta of her luxury bedroom.

She was eager for a whirlpool bath, hot water running over her skin, soap bubbles in her hair.

Her dreams burst as her mother announced breaking news while driving with tedious obedience to all traffic laws as she transported her daughter from the base back to Tyler.

"I had to report him missing no matter what the consequences."

"So Dad has taken a hike." Bonita did not seem surprised. "And our house is a crime scene. Great."

"Only for tonight. They will be searching. They won't find anything. Then we can go home tomorrow."

"Great," Bonita repeated.

"I'll need a fix at the club tonight. I need to see men. I can take your things with me, if you need." Marlotta made this announcement to her daughter, who had brought little from camp. "You'll have to stay at a hotel or rent a bed at the library."

"Rent a bed at the library?" Bonita laughed derisively.

"They do that now. Much cheaper than a hotel, but not nearly as much space. Just a bed behind a curtain unless you purchase an experience."

"I'd like to experience The Men Unadorned Club."

"I'm sorry you are not old enough to go."

"Old enough to serve my country but not to patronize the family business." She repositioned her rucksack and gun case, both in the front seat with the two women.

"Hush. You are never to speak of that! No one knows who owns the club. It is confidential information."

"Why do we have to keep it a secret? I don't understand. It is a respectable enterprise. No cameras. No ice cream. No smartphones."

"It is socially risky to let people know you own a business. Plus, we are branching out into time travel."

"Oh," said Bonita. "No, wait. I still don't understand. The

military is investigating time travel as a way to preempt incursions. No results yet. I'm dying to get into such a futuristic program if I can qualify."

Marlotta cut her eyes. "You'd do well to stay away from that program. Train for educational supervision duty or the bomb disposal unit."

"I intend to work in a field that interests me. Time travel research has a future."

"And possibly a past," said Marlotta. "You just have to accept what I tell you. Time travel is new. It has social repercussions which are not apparent yet."

"You mean something like unintended consequences?"

"Yes. If it goes sour, we are going to dump it as soon as possible. We cannot have The Men Unadorned Club tainted by a failure."

"Failing won't deter the government."

"The government does not have to worry about making a profit. We could lose our shirts."

"So why get into it at all?"

"The prospect of real money. If everything goes right, we could make billions. It's win or lose. So you have to accept what I say."

"I don't have to accept anything. I make plenty as a soldier. I don't need to be involved in the business."

"You won't be young forever. If you don't exercise your Death Option before you turn 45, you'll be retired from active duty and they will cut your income in half."

"That's a long way away. And don't worry. I'm not as stupid as Aunt Carlotta. I've no intention of exercising a Death Option of my own free will."

"Your Aunt Carlotta wanted to undertake a journey in her profession that would resonate throughout the ages."

"She journeyed into the path of a guillotine blade. I've always been suspicious if she actually intended to do that."

"Absolutely she did. Carlotta's exercising of her Death Option while starring in such a classic film as the *Twilight of the French*

50

South, a movie that no one who ever saw it can ever forget, ensured she would remain forever young."

"And forever gone."

"Unfortunately we profited little from her demise, having lost the rights to her image to the anti-French Dixie groups that claimed the drama capitalized on the misfortune of the war's victims."

"There haven't been any war movies made since that Supreme Court Decision, holding any terrorism property damage connected to the movie's subject as the responsibility of the film's participants, all of them, even down to the janitors on the sets."

"Those janitors could have stopped it!" declared Bonita.

"You don't understand, it was a tragedy. For us and the First Amendment."

"My fellow soldiers and I feel slighted since no scripts or literature about us will ever be filmed no matter how heroic we are," Bonita admitted.

"Is that why there are so many who exercise their Death Options in war games? I hope you don't plan on any such action."

"Never fear, Mother, I don't intend to. I shall grow old if I can."

"Everyone fears that in the next life we will look exactly like we do at the instant of departure in this one. At least Carlotta will have the assurance she will never look old."

"I've heard the theory we look the absolute best we ever looked here when we get there."

"I don't know. Some say we have a choice."

"I will definitely choose the way I look now. I cannot possibly get any better looking as I grow old."

"You believe that? Some say that older people look better as the years pass."

Bonita laughed.

"Don't you believe it, Mother. I know you changed your appearance so that you don't automatically look like an older version of Aunt Carlotta."

"Nobody can conceive your Aunt Carlotta any way but young. Occasionally someone remarks I must have resembled her when I was young. I just tell them no, I looked much different when I was younger."

And all I did was darken my hair and purchase dark frame eyeglasses. And grow older…

Defensive to her daughter, Marlotta raged inwardly, still questioning all the decisions she had ever made about her personal life, wishing she was still at the club...

Outwardly she was calm.

"Maybe you will get to look like yourself again after you die."

"We cannot be sure what form we will take in the next life. As I said, it's a long way off for me, leaving the service or dying for that matter."

In her peripheral vision, Marlotta surveyed her 16-year-old daughter, not for the first time discerning the characteristic family stubbornness, undeveloped until the girl was accepted into the army at the minimum service age of 14.

"Not as long as you foresee. You could be forced into a premature aging program if you have any illness or accidents. And they haven't invented a way to stop the years from passing yet."

"Now it is not easy to get into the time research program. They prefer people who are 18 so they can apply to legally change their age and be older if needed."

"I'd care to know who's behind that," said Marlotta.

"Same agency investigating time travel, I suspect. And if that one succeeds then we won't have to grow older. They expect to stop time in its tracks."

Marlotta sighed. "Then your father would never return. I figured you'd be more concerned."

"He's probably just run off with another woman," Bonita said reflectively.

"I suppose you would not blame him."

"Mother, you know I am always on your side."

"Are you?"

"Yes. We're alike, you know. What did the police say?"

"Oh, I don't know. It was the weekend. The car was still in the shop. I just faxed a missing person's notification in triplicate."

"Seems a bit drastic they wanted to search the house so quickly."

"I thought so. But he's a deliverer. So it went straight to a captain. A Captain Parks."

"Do you think Dad might be dead?"

"I- I doubt that. Maybe."

"If so, the government is also researching exactly what does happen after we pass on. If he left some testimony it could help me get into that research program."

"Bonita, I think you should wait and see what how this turns out."

"I could make major in no time!" *Unless they find me out...*

"But you are only a private!"

"Nothing is impossible," declared Bonita.

"Except you coming to the club tonight. I have a spot where I can sleep there."

"You do?"

"Yes, in one of the role-play sets."

Bonita narrowed her eyes at her mother, felt her weapon, but did not reply.

"So should I take you to the library?"

"I have enough money for a hotel. I'll keep all my gear with me. Screw the library. I'd rather sleep in a coffin."

Chapter 12

Raize Parks contemplated the missing person's report on his desk.

This was serious.

An employee of the highest paying occupation in civil service, next to police and fire.

Raize's superior was going to command instant results.

Society designated the missing man as his socioeconomic peer- a package carrier, commonly called a deliverer. Referred to as mailmen in the remote past, the valued professionals who delivered packages and letters to residences and businesses were drawn from the elite of society.

Police and fire personnel had legitimate Death Options, with strong incentive to exercise them under numerous circumstances.

As the glue which bonded society, deliverers had no such obligations.

Shopping was accomplished by the one-way screen installed in all dwellings. Shoppers placed their orders by touch from a selection of stores of their choice.

Deliverers brought their purchases to their homes.

Most deliverers worked days. Only emergency deliveries were made at night.

The fortunate few received high pay, government provided uniforms, excellent benefits, and had no exercisable Death Option.

Therefore, it ranked as the profession of choice for many. Selection was strict. Only the best.

This man, Lars Holt, appeared unimpeachable.

Educated, married, a father.

Army veteran.

Family man.

Admired by all.

Raize contemplated contacting his man undercover at The Men Unadorned Club about Lars Holt.

The establishment headed the list of locations receiving packages personally from the murdered man.

54

The FBI suspected The Men Unadorned Club was also operating as a fraudulent time travel portal.

"In the last five years several Tyler area people have vanished right before or after supposed time travel experiences rumored connected to the club. The FBI is not buying the company's explanation that the missing have gotten lost in the past, either by accident or on purpose. They suspect foul play," Raize had reported to his agent six months ago.

"Here in the present?"

"Of course, here in the present! Don't be smart."

"And that is the reason I am about to become a nude dancer?" Loyce Landers had replied.

"Yes. After much work the FBI has narrowed down common elements. The persons who disappeared all had three things in common. They investigated but did not purchase Time Travel experiences. They all had excellent reasons to vanish. They or their wives or girlfriends all had been to The Men Unadorned Club as patrons."

"I'm taking my clothes off now," Loyce had replied, and facetiously removed his tie and unbuttoned his shirt.

Raize had laughed then.

He was not laughing now.

New to the Tyler area, unknown to most in the department, Loyce Landers had successfully infiltrated the club.

Only Raize knew who Loyce Landers really was. He had become an expert performer.

While a rookie, Loyce Lee Landers, was a valuable young attractive police officer. He had served recently in the military, working with special operations. He also was not too different in social status from the male murder victim.

Lars Holt was a senior deliverer, responsible for packages arriving the same day as ordered or next day for a few choice businesses and government agencies.

The Men Unadorned Club was on that list.

The missing deliverer had shown no interest in time travel and no one had a motive to want him gone.

Raize dismissed the idea of jeopardizing Loyce Landers' cover for an unplanned liaison just yet. It was safe enough for Loyce to contact Raize but for Raize to initiate a communiqué was dangerous.

Secondly, Raize contemplated calling Electra Simpson about this latest disappearance.

Again he held off, mainly because he had no evidence that Lars Holt met the criteria for FBI involvement.

However if he suspected any suspicious activity at The Men Unadorned Club linked to the dead deliverer, Raize could petition the agency for help.

Without the tool of surveillance footage, necessarily outlawed in tandem with cameras, it would take hours, if not days, to ascertain if Lars Holt had been there. A snap search of the man's residence had yielded nothing except a forbidden formal gown in a teenage daughter's room.

Not even worth confiscating.

He was pressed to identify a promising line of inquiry.

Electra's time was valuable. He would be blamed if she spent her days tracking a red herring.

Still, he needed to tell Loyce or Electra soon.

This was too much responsibility for one man alone.

Electra Simpson solved the problem for him with her unannounced entrance into his office.

"I am a police official," he said mildly.

She swept in with a flounce and landed noisily in the chair.

"You think you need warning before I appear?"

He grinned at her. He liked Electra at this moment. She was down to earth and practical in a technological world.

At 50 years of age, she recalled the same lifestyle of youth as him.

She had lived it also.

An era before the technology explosion…

He wished he more than liked Electra.

He perceived she anticipated more from the relationship also.

Yet neither had made a move.

Although she gave him an encouraging smile right now.

"Electra, I have another missing person."

She jumped right in. "A deliverer. It is already in the wind. There may be few VIPs left but many VICs- very important careers. So I've been briefed."

"So you know about Lars Holt? I'm not surprised."

"I know. I got a call from my boss this morning. Apparently he had been looking into a Time Travel experience. But he had not booked anything."

"That would be an anomaly."

"Yes sirree! Deviating from the pattern. And on top of that, no connection to Men Unadorned."

"Wrong. They are on his route list."

"No kidding! But I have another for you. I've been letting every missing Tyler area person's file flit across my FBI screen lately. A young student, high school student, has also been reported missing. Right?"

"So? Dozens of them in the Tyler area. Which one?"

"A Magdalene Rene Watters. Just 17. Reported by her grandparents."

Raize was silent a moment. He did not want Electra to know he had broken protocol and actually spoken to the grandparents about the FBI and what role the bureau could play in their dilemma.

"Hmm, that would not even get to me. It would be assigned to some lieutenant. Oh wait! That was the one I told you about. I forget why it came to my attention. I sent it back to a patrol officer."

"Well, get it away from him or her. Magdalene Rene Watters knew Lars Holt."

"Knew him?"

"Yep. As a deliverer, Holt is required to do 11 hours of community service each year. He did his last stint at her high school a few months ago. Reports are she worked with him to gain her required community service hours for graduation."

"What did they do?"

"A humanitarian project with six other students. Rounded up stray cats and raised money to get them fixed. I talked to some of the other students and the two of them hit it off real good."

"So? They would not have been alone together? Oh, hell. I forget there are no more teachers. Another modern innovation."

"I don't know about that. But with only a minimum wage chaperon watching, bored and from a distance, I would not count it out. Replacing classroom teachers with remote controlled computers was a bad mistake, if you ask me. But nobody asked me. So getting back to this missing deliverer, I feel there is a good chance something developed between him and the girl."

"Are you suggesting a married deliverer would risk his family, career, his life even, to enter into a relationship with a 16-year-old?"

"It happens. Lower class as she was, he could have been a natural attraction for her. According to her records, she tested as smart. Had potential."

"Still. I cannot imagine a man wanting someone younger than him."

"It happens, I tell you. Sometimes it is just sex. All he wants is his exterior in a younger interior. Sometimes not. Maybe they fell in love."

"How could they get away with it? How could they get together?"

"Well, Magdalene Watters did not live near the Holt residence if you navigate by street map. But if she happened to be enterprising enough she could easily walk through the city park and be almost in the backyard of her lover's house."

"That must be how they kept it a secret. Never leaving a trail. We need to take note."

Electra laughed but Raize wondered whether she was joking.

Raize scanned Electra's figure as she stood. She was handsome for her age. He suspected she had a hard time keeping her weight within legisled limits. Nevertheless, even keeping just below the official standard for her height, she presented an acceptable body build.

Both of them single, it would be so convenient for them to fall in love…

It had not happened.

Despite mutual admiration, compatibility, interests- all the elements needed.

It had not happened.

But it could, still.

"Let's keep this investigation close to us," he said. "Let's work on it together."

Electra nodded, almost absentmindedly, as if that had been a foregone conclusion.

"Begin at the beginning," she said.

They looked at a list of people to interview about the disappearance of Lars Holt.

"This is his wife, Marlotta."

Something about her driver's license photo looked vaguely familiar but Raize could not place it. He pointed this out to Electra.

"She resembles somebody."

"Your imagination," Electra said.

"Some sports star, maybe."

"Did you interview her?"

"Hmm." Raize picked up a photograph of the younger girl. "No, she just phoned in a report. Left a message."

"And the daughter, Bonita?"

"Not really a suspect. But there is this one."

And there was a picture of an attractively plain young woman, with frizzy gray/brown hair, no makeup, wearing dark rimmed glasses.

Manager of The Men Unadorned Club, Amy Raxel.

"Why her?" asked Electra.

"Might have had regular interaction with the deliverer."

"No coworkers of the missing man to interview?"

"No colleagues from the Delivery Service would know Lars Holt. He worked from home and answered to an out of town superior via direct connection. He retrieved his packages from a robotic belt and posted them to the same."

"Someone had to service his vehicle occasionally." Electra snapped her fingers.

"Great, let's divide as follows. You take the wife and daughter. I'll take the manager and the mechanic."

"Perfect."

Raize held out his hand. "Let's go eat and strategize about this."

Electra smiled. "Okay! Done deal!"

As they were preparing to exit his office, Raize had another recollection.

"One of my sergeants was complaining about being bugged by a cat whisperer trying to convince him one of her kitty clients had witnessed a murder or two."

Despite their senior level officials in a social structure that embraced animals as near human, they both burst into laughter.

Electra recovered first.

"Those damn whisperers. I don't care what science says, I know they are all frauds."

"You and me both. However, I do recall my sergeant saying the murders were of an older man who had just had sex with a young girl. That's what stuck in his mind. I'll have to call him and see if there could be any link."

"I agree. Whatever he reports, you had better talk to the whisperer and see what she says."

"She's surely crazy. Thinks she can talk to cats."

"Or, if there's anything to it, she did it," Electra agreed.

The couple left, each thinking what a fine start to an even better evening to come.

Chapter 13

Why can't I feel for Electra Simpson what I feel right now?

Raize Parks hoped his arousal at the sight of the cat whisperer was not obvious to the woman with fragile aura of mystery clinging to her as dust to a statue.

His dinner with Electra had been engaging, intellectually stimulating, and a pleasure in every way.

He could summon no sexual attraction to her.

He had tried…

At the end of the date, he had kissed her on the cheek and they had headed in separate directions, to meet again in a professional capacity the next day.

Nothing had changed.

Then this woman, Debriah Brock, had walked into his office and identified herself as the cat whisperer who had talked with his sergeant.

Raize's eyebrows arched. His tongue rolled over his teeth. He used eclectic methods to do his detecting, using any and all available resources from DNA to psychic analysis. On the latter however, he was a cynic, prone to questioning any claim not scientifically provable.

However, he was not entirely trusting of science either.

The cat whisperer seemed not to be aware of Raize, other than his capacity as an authority figure willing to listen to her story.

He was engrossed, listening with his fingers together at the tips, trying to focus on her words rather than the sensations of desire and the intense longing he felt.

He knew legally she was too young for him.

There existed more than 10 years between them.

Yet instantly a great hunger for her arose.

Desire settled over Debriah also. She had the uneasy feeling it was almost visible.

Like haze on a sunlit river.

The man before her took her back to her teenage years.

She saw the same kind eyes she had once beheld when her first lover caressed her. A familiar comfort and sense of safety warmed her.

Less animated and more refined than her lost love, nevertheless the same type of man.

Moreover, at once she trusted him completely.

Debriah found herself telling him more than she had planned. As she detailed her story, her focus shifted slightly, her natural inclination to put others first emerged.

She remained aware of Raize as a man but at the presenting moment her concern spilled out for two dead lovers she had never even met.

At least she believed they were dead.

She tried passionately to convey that faith to Raize Parks.

"I know my profession is not held in high esteem by all law enforcement officials," she said perceptively. "Please understand that I am a naturalist. I don't believe talking to animals can be taught. I was born with the ability."

"So you don't hold the DNA experiments accountable for your, um, exotic talent?"

"Let's not talk politics. Doesn't matter how I got the ability. I have it."

"And psychic ability?"

She bit her lip. She knew skeptics considered whisperers less suspicious than psychics.

Yet something deep inside her longed to reveal her true talent to this man.

To let him see her as she was.

So he could accept her or reject her truly.

Despite the fact that he was an officer of the law, she was eerily tempted to tell him about her only illegal activity.

To admit she was the member of a banned society and let the chips fall where they may.

"Weren't you a registered psychic until just recently?" Captain Parks chewed unconsciously on a pen while he waited for her reply.

Not only that, I'm a member of The Society of Displaced

Christians, she wanted to blurt out to him.

"Miss?"

Would you be interested, I wonder?

Debriah emerged from her fantasy of confessing her social sins to this police officer. She would jeopardize her profession. Being a cat whisperer and a Christian at the same time also violated the Conflict of Belief law.

"I'm sorry. I lost track. This has been disconcerting. What were you asking?"

"You were a licensed psychic previously. Why did you not renew your license?"

"I rejected psychic work."

"I was taught psychics had no choice. You are born that way, I was taught. Same as right handed or left handed. Same as gay or straight. Same as dog lover or cat lover."

"The courts did not agree with that theory."

"I'm aware of that. I disagree. Just my opinion."

"Whatever you believe, we don't have to use our abilities if we don't care to."

That was not wholly true. It was hard to ignore feelings and revelations.

Debriah was having such a conflict right now.

She saw herself in this man's arms, in his bed, naked next to him. She shook herself, trying to hear his words rather than imagine his body.

"I was saying it is hard for someone like me to simply take the word of a person whose source is a cat."

"I don't blame you."

Debriah focused his face. He had kind eyes. Tired, but kind. She tried to stem emotions exploding as endearment.

She was failing.

"Could you give me the address of where the, um, cat says this took place?"

"That's part of the limitation. She doesn't know where she was, I mean. Of course, she distinguished where she was but cats incorporate environments differently. She cannot directly tell me where she was in a way I can understand. And this is an exceptionally talented feline, with high communication skills."

"Her ancestors involved in the DNA experiment?"

"No. Perhaps you would care to meet Carousel. Her person is letting her stay with me for a few days. I haven't told the owner anything except Carousel is dangerously stressed. I did not know what to do or say. I was just hoping someone would take it seriously. It is real, I know it is."

"I have never met with a feline material witness before. I am not sure how to proceed."

"First you have to get permission."

Raize looked blank.

"Permission?"

"Yes, just like children. You need the owner's permission to speak with an animal."

Speak with an animal.

Raize recalled days of hardship and deprivation. A withdrawal of the mind so severe he could still feel the sting of the sunlight every dawn.

He had rejected that past when he received his calling as a detective.

He had come out of that darkness into the light of reason.

To live a life of purpose and fulfillment.

To be of service to others as a police officer.

Now he had to interview a cat.

With foreboding, he recognized his past enticing him.

Chapter 14

"He took me to see the jails."

The next day Debriah had been unable to keep it to herself, walking over to Samantha's house that evening.

"OH, that sounds so romantic." Samantha rolled her eyes.

"Oddly it was. They were empty, of course. Down long winding hallways, I would've been lost if he had not been there. Once when we were alone on the way, he stopped and turned to me. He kissed me gently."

"What next?"

"Oh, nothing really."

Samantha had enumerated every memorable detail of her own encounter with Loyce Smith the next day after that relationship began.

Debriah was not sure she wanted to share everything.

She stopped speaking to Samantha but the memory continued in her mind.

After the gentle kiss in the hallway, Raize and Debriah had returned to his office where they were now alone.

She found herself behind his desk, standing before him as he lounged comfortably in a chair.

Anticipating additional paperwork connected with her statement was just a delusion on her part.

She knew it.

At the same time she did not know it.

Was not sure what was next. Would it be a kiss?

He knew…

Slowly, before she comprehended what he was doing, he reached up with his left hand and began caressing her stomach.

Delicately at first, then she began to feel his touch more.

Totally struck, totally stunned, she felt shock, a little frightened, but most of all delighted.

She made up her mind right then, not to stop him, knowing the implication of that lack of action.

"Do you want me to stop?" he whispered. All the while he had been glancing behind her every now and then, in case anybody walked towards the office.

Somehow, she indicated no.

What was wrong with this man?

An attractive man like him could have his choice among mature attractive seasoned women.

Women who would not jeopardize his very life.

Or maybe he had so many of those he was tired of them. No, she did not believe it.

An illegal relationship with an older man. Could she?

What frightened her most was, while she was at the beginning of this, she knew it was going to have to have an end.

Someday that would hurt.

She would have to prepare for him vanishing from her life from the beginning.

His hands were so soft and gentle.

She fought them only superficially and her body twisted, thrilling at his touch.

He became calm. Still gently caressing her,

"I would like to touch your neck," Raize whispered to Debriah.

"I don't know." She looked down, still needing to stall him.

"Oh, say yes, Debriah! Please say yes," he begged.

"I'm overwhelmed. I never expected this."

"Have you ever had a man's lips on your neck?"

"Never."

The only man Debriah had ever truly known in the carnal way had been uninterested in unnatural sexual activity.

"Then you are a neck virgin."

He was excited visibly now and he showed a little teeth as he bent towards her.

She grabbed him and pulled him close.

His lips on her neck caused electric sensations up and down her spine.

But they had to part.

Others in the building stirred outside his office.

"Let me give you my address."

She wrote it down with directions to her house.

Now at Samantha's house, after a day full of distracting patrons, plus mentoring to Carousel in between, Debriah was mentally reliving the beginning of her love affair.

She jumped on Samantha's client couch and had the lid to the sofa pulled as far down as it would go without snapping shut.

"Why are you wearing that high collar as hot as it?" Samantha asked.

Debriah was beginning to suspect her best friend was less than approving. "I am trying to be in style."

"Your encounter with the esteemed officer did not leave tooth marks, did it?' Samantha leaned her professional chair back.

"As far as Captain Parks, he is devoted to helping Carousel."

Samantha popped the sofa lid wide open.

"An animal devotee, huh? Just the kind of guy you need to have an illicit affair with. Loyce is devoted to me. We are going to be married and we are going to produce children." She grinned.

Debriah rose up, leaning partway out of the sofa, over the side.

"Samantha! I hope you realize who does all the production work. Analyze the risks!"

"Sure you are not just jealous because you are too young to wed Raize Parks? You are the one taking a risk. Beware of police and firefighters and people with personalities that lead to such employment. The professional peer pressure on the occupations that come with Death Options are too strong for some people."

"I'm sure our relationship is just temporary. And you must not tell anyone. He is risking capital punishment if we get caught. That's what makes it so exciting!"

"I won't tell anyone. Loyce swore me to secrecy about us, too. I don't know why. Maybe his employers prefer their entertainers unattached."

"At least nude dancing jobs don't come with Death Options."

"Amen to that. Speaking of death, what about the murders? Heard anything? Has your friend told you about the investigation?"

"Only that they cannot find any bodies. Even if they do they have to make sure those unfortunate people weren't exercising a voluntary Death Option."

"And the choice is so- so- emotional. Almost irrational at times. I don't know how they would be able to tell sometimes. The personality traits behind accepting the Death Option are not examined closely enough."

Debriah regarded Samantha silently for a second. She was reflecting that her friend was not as far away from the psychology she had studied, then rejected, as claimed.

"So you are sure about Loyce."

"Absolutely. I guess my days of clubbing are over. It's to the library for me when I want to relieve stress…"

Samantha smiled.

"Don't forget to put my name down as referral," Debriah said.

Chapter 15

He cannot be tainted with vampirism. It must have been an undercover assignment. This is the man I'm going to marry. It cannot be true.

Electra Simpson stared at her FBI computer screen in disbelief. Files accessed only by knowing secret government codes revealed Raize Parks, a respected police captain, had an ominous past. Her eyes boring into the flat LED image, she recalled the life of fame and fortune she had turned away in order to serve the cause of justice.

She had survived many hardships and passed many excruciating tests, mental and physical to follow her chosen path.

Meeting Raize Parks had seemed to endorse that choice.

He appeared perfect. Devoted for almost two decades to police work, a respectable person, sincere and honest, tough minded and thoroughly diligent in his job.

He had never married and had no children.

Computerized sexual tests had yielded the same result over and over.

They were almost one hundred percent matched.

Tolerantly, Electra did allow for some small margin of error, as she had filled in Raize's portion of the tests herself, without him knowing anything about it, since he had no clearance to access any computer files.

She had been sure she knew him well enough to fill in all the blanks about him in the test forms.

Now, acting on an unanticipated outlandish tip, she had dug up evidence of a murky and salacious history.

This was not fair!

How could this be her reward?

Electra quickly killed the monitor as a clerk walked into the office.

Scanning the confidential personnel files of colleagues was against the law even if she had received an anonymous tip. Electra had violated the rules on a whim, hoping she would unearth something to better connect with Raize Parks.

Some small bit of knowledge which would enable her to advance in his eyes. In addition, refute the tipster with acumen.

Instead she had found his career had a dark origin.

A practicing vampire, using an assumed name, turned informer, turned respected cop.

That last turn would ruin him if it became common knowledge among his police colleagues.

She could let no one know what she had read. The penalty would be her own job, if not her freedom.

Nevertheless, she would not be able to erase the label from her brain.

Practicing vampire.

The only redeeming idea was that inserting such material in Raize's file was prelude to a major undercover operation yet to begin.

Therefore, false.

Fiction.

Had to be.

Electra consoled herself with a silver lining.

If the wild details in the file did turn out to be true, it would be hard for Raize to refuse her proposals.

What am I thinking? I don't want to blackmail him into a partnership with me...

The clerk finished his task and left the office.

Electra flipped the monitor back on and saved the file to a flash drive.

There was no reason not to hope the relationship would not progress on the track she anticipated.

The flash drive would keep.

And she hoped it would not be needed.

She slipped the device in her purse with her gun.

Trying to take her mind off the problem, Electra perused the written file on her desk.

The Men Unadorned Club.

Electra laughed with irony.

Image me being assigned to investigate that!

Nude men flashed before her eyes. Remnants of naked males

she had seen and many she had imagined…

Electra grabbed her coat, hat, and purse.

A night at The Men Unadorned Club was just what she needed.

Chapter 16

Out of the corner of his eye, Loyce was surprised to glimpse Electra Simpson arriving at The Men Unadorned Club.

He knew she would not recognize him.

She lounged at a stage side table and ordered a drink. He witnessed one of the new hires approach.

Wonder what she thinks of a man without any hair anywhere? Loyce mused.

Electra stood up and walked away with the rookie dancer. Tempted to follow, Loyce was more interested in the small office occupied by Amy Raxel.

Investigating her was his goal for the evening. He decided to stick to it. Electra and her acquaintance left Loyce's field of vision as he moved towards the administrative area of the club.

Amy Raxel was off this night.

He took the chance to slip into her office unnoticed. He was hoping to swipe some clothing. A large china cabinet occupied an entire sidewall of the room.

He opened the doors. Surprisingly it was empty. No clothes of any variety, not even any garment bags.

Then he saw.

The entire back panel of the cabinet was an entryway.

He gave it a push.

It opened into a surprisingly large hall where there were numerous people hurrying back and forth.

The hall was lit with a minimum of light. Nevertheless, he knew he was going to stand out.

All these people, including the men, had on layers of clothing…

Always adept at finding a corner from which to spy, Loyce hid in a small partition that fed into the wide hallway, which he soon visually ascertained accessed numerous small rooms.

Unfortunately, he found no attire of any kind behind the partition.

Loyce decided to emerge, regardless. He could always say he

got confused about the doors and was trying to get to his room.

"You there!"

Loyce heard someone come through the cabinet behind him.

"You there, are you supposed to be in the next experience?"

"Yes, mam."

"Are you a German, Britain, or on our side?"

The middle-aged woman pulled him out into the hall.

She was wearing an 1800s period costume. She laughed as she looked him up and down.

"Didn't they give you any clothes? They don't usually start the extras off naked. You should have been given your costume in the inner office."

"Actually they informed me I was going to be nude in the experience."

"Oh, well, I guess it's because you are so cute."

The woman strategically pulled his hair in jest.

"Follow me," she said.

And she took off ahead of him.

It was hard to tell but Loyce was sure this was the same woman he often saw in the front row of tables in the performance area.

She looked like the one who had commented on his weight.

Yet she was very different in costume.

This woman was emotional and passionate as she demonstrated in one of the small rooms off the hall.

No wonder those costumes are banned in most of the world. They do effect a personality change.

"So I guess when the client comes in, you are to immediately begin to have sex with her. She will be slightly under the influence of opioids."

"What else do I do?"

"Didn't they tell you anything? We are giving her a Time Travel experience. We must convince her she is back in time in the midst of the war, making love to a soldier. Then we will come in and shoot you. I will be playing my part at the end as I always do. Surely they told you that."

"Of course," Loyce had lied. "I just wanted to make sure I please the client."

"This woman is just for the exotic sexual thrill. She wants a satisfactory exterior inside her interior. I guess that's why you didn't get a costume. Also don't mention South America. She might get ideas and that costs a lot extra. I'm going to get some more props and find you a costume to get into if the woman doesn't respond to you well. But before I abandon you to another, I want you to rehearse just a little."

And the woman took off the voluminous dress and extensive undergarments faster than he imagined possible.

She was beautiful for her age. Her thin frame had only a slightly rounded abdomen and minor creeping of her skin. Her breasts, while sagging, were supple with huge nipples.

Loyce rehearsed with enthusiasm.

When recollections of Samantha flitted across his mind, the idea that this was all in the line of duty followed in line like a freight train.

Finishing and redressing, the woman promised to return as soon as possible.

"I'd prefer another rehearsal before the client arrives but I'd better get the props and your costume first."

Flagrant violation of the rules and laws outraged Loyce but he was unsure if what he had just encountered was outright illegal or just some type of ethically immoral fraud.

Soon after the woman left, after a short inner debate over the merits of another rehearsal verses the possible dangers of staying, Loyce escaped from the room.

Chapter 17

"The key to what goes on here appears to be a possible proprietor who masquerades as a customer. I've been shadowing her every chance I get." Loyce Landers whispered into the payphone.

He was reporting to Raize Parks.

"Sorry I didn't learn any more. I didn't take to the part about being shot at the end," he told Raize.

He had omitted detailing the rehearsal to his boss but was careful to give him all other pertinent observations in as few words as possible.

"There's the regular set of offices off the foyer opposite the performance area. In there is a door marked 'closet' but it is not a closet. That's the hall to the private quarters they provide the employees. The manager's office is a separate enclosed small partition. Inside it is a huge old cabinet, concealing a doorway to a different hall."

Raize looked at his phone and shook his head.

He recognized the name of the manager.

Such a coincidence was suspect at once.

"So this woman's office has a secret entrance concealed inside a china cabinet. Does she know about it herself?"

"That's an excellent question. She might not. She's out on the floor most of the time and this seems to be accessed after hours."

"Tell me more about this cabinet," he instructed Loyce.

"Down that hall there's a hidden maze of rooms in the building accessible only by that cabinet."

"You are sure? A door inside a cabinet? You weren't participating in one of their time travel experiences?"

"I have not had any drugs. It's a giant old antique china cabinet. Back panel is a door in disguise."

"Creative. A door leading to hall with a labyrinth of rooms?"

"Correct. I managed to get in through the cabinet and I saw evidence of French Dixie activities."

"That explains a lot! So these people are French Dixie War reenactors? In a hidden complex? Drama with a sex element? Or more? Terrorists possibly?"

"Not sure yet how deep it goes. She did ask whether I was British or German. And the remark about South America. It all fits."

Raize's excitement ballooned as Loyce continued.

The French Dixie War, which had eclipsed the American Civil War of the 1860s as the most studied and analyzed war in western civilization, was only three decades ago.

The war was quick but bloody. Over 2 million French men and women fell in renovated World War I trenches in a one-year escalation of the conflict. Non-fatal injuries approached five million.

As the carnage in the French Dixie war progressed, other European powers had felt the compulsion to take arms against the French. The Germans and British had joined forced, invaded France, and restored order by putting French Dixie opponents in power.

The new French government exiled French Dixie supporters to countries on the Arabian Peninsula.

Some escaped to South America, some to North Africa, others made it to Las Vegas.

"And the remark about South America. That means it could be more than just role-play. Suppose that explains the disappearances? A terrorism link?"

"Possibly. I don't know what else it could be. As I made my way back down the hall I heard a lot of background noise behind the other doors and there were gunshots."

"Gunshots?"

"Yes, probably not real, but I could not be sure. And I caught snippets of the conversations as I went by. Some of the talking exposed supposed traitors to the movement."

"Implying loyalty to the French Dixie cause?"

Federal terrorist crimes popped like power points in Raize's brain.

"I never actually heard that term. But I was not staying to listen."

"What else did you see?"

"Several people stepped out of the various doors, some appeared drunk. All were dressed as if living in the 1800s. You know if they claim they were reenacting the American Civil War instead of the French Dixie War, they can get away with it under the Freedom of Antique Expression Act."

"No one is interested in American Civil War reenactments any more. No one is interested in that conflict, period. That happened so long ago it might as well have been in the stone ages."

The old American Southern ideals were a threat of nearly 200 years ago.

In present times any signs of support for the French Dixie cult in the US, including portraying the actual creators of the conflict in a positive way, constituted terrorism under law.

Fictional characters were a gray area.

This was the bill that originally provoked a backlash in the entertainment industry, resulting in classic films, such as the one that had made Carlotta Fortune a posthumous cult icon despite the fact that she had nothing to do with the real war, being suppressed.

Pursuing French Dixie supporters became a slippery political slope for authorities when the members of the movement began to protest under the first amendment.

Then the monetary punishment stopped Hollywood cold. All profits from anything related to the era had to go to war victims.

There were still frequent court cases about individual acts, with rulings skewed in both directions, sometimes letting French Dixie activism legally slide.

However, if there were actual violent crimes committed in their name, it was much easier to take them down.

"Any indication of anyone injured or dead?" Raize asked hopefully.

"No. Everybody acted happy and looked healthy. A couple of women snatched at me as I was getting back into the china cabinet but I made excuses and fended them off. I waited until all was silent in the offices, slipped out and made my way back to the performance area."

"Damn. If they are doing illegal reenactments, it could be serious or nothing at all. You must learn more. Keep quiet for now."

"French Dixie terrorism is the domain of the FBI. I'm not that familiar with the background."

"I'm afraid I never completely followed all the history behind the French Dixie controversy either. But most people don't. They just know about the current terroristic threats and to steer clear if they want to avoid trouble."

"I know. But French Dixieism doesn't scare me."

"Me neither. And I don't intend to let the FBI take this over if I can help it. We'll do all the work and they'll take all the credit."

"Great. I agree. But, did you know Electra Simpson was here?"

Raize caught his breath.

Electra did not know Loyce Landers' identity. Raize was delaying telling her, hoping to keep Loyce's presence an absolute secret for the present.

But Loyce knew who Electra was. He had her contact information in case anything happened to Raize.

Instructed by Raize to remain in the shadows at the office and memorize her features, he had observed the FBI agent in detail when she visited Raize one day before his assignment had begun.

"Of course Electra Simpson would be there. On duty, no doubt. When she is there do not approach her. Let her do her job the way she needs to. Just stay in touch with me and try to find out more."

"Right. Try to let me know a little more about the movement. There's something about a movie and some famous dead actress."

"Yeah. But that all happened years ago. It's the clothing style that is important. That is there weakness. They dress like that whenever they can get away with it. You know the look?"

"Certainly."

"One more thing. I recognized the name of the manager. She may be involved in something else recently brought to my attention."

"Oh?"

"You say she works right in front of this hidden section but you are not sure she goes in or knows anything about it. You are sure Amy Raxel is her name?"

"Correct. Amy Raxel. The door marked 'closet' is in her office. Until I realized what that meant I thought she knew nothing about anything. One of those hear no evil, see no evil, loyal blind employees. Now I'm not so sure. And there are rumors around here that she is a practicing vampire. Nobody believes it. She is so plain. Is that the other matter?"

Raize's heart skipped a beat.

"No, it's something else. Let's try to keep vampirism out of it," said Raize firmly. "If we build our case on vampirism and vampirism is legalized, as it soon may be, then we have nothing. Let's stick to the idea that this is only prohibited reenactment for right now. Get more facts. We need to identify any French Dixie sympathizers."

"What do you want me to do next?"

"I'm leaving you a package. I managed to secure a manually activated recording chip. I know you're familiar with those from your military work. I want you to implant it and use it if necessary."

"How did you manage to get your hands on one of those? They are banned except for the FBI and higher level government agencies."

"I know. But remember I have a friend at the FBI."

Raize bit his lip. He was not exactly lying to Loyce.

However, the captain was afraid the law and order devotee would not use the chip if he knew that Raize had skillfully lifted it from Electra's supplies while at her office for a consultation.

Without her knowledge or permission, he exulted with some pride.

"Okay. I will feel safer with that chip to back me up. Does the device send data back to its original processor or to a remote location?"

"No. It is a classified entity so I'm afraid it is only going to record, not send any sound waves to anyone. That function had to be disabled within its system settings. It will only record like an old 20th century cassette tape recorder. Only a miniature version. But as soon as you get anything audible that gives up any pertinent information, call me. I can put the device in a decoder and listen to everything it picks up within a 10 feet range."

"I'll insert the chip as soon as I receive it."

"Great. I will track down Amy Raxel and question her as soon as possible. And remember, don't talk about vampirism. It is Dixie French activities we are interested in. And locating the missing people. Go through that china cabinet again as soon as you can."

"Right. I will not hesitate, believe me."

Chapter 18

"I know why you are here." Amy Raxel offered Raize Parks a muffin.

"No, thank you, I'm on duty." Raize looked over Amy with a surreptitious eye.

Attractively plain. Smooth white neck, pale brown frizzy hair, dark rimmed glasses, ruby red lipstick and bright teeth.

Both third teeth were pointed.

She was a practicing vampire and he knew it.

She had recognized the signs in him at first sight. Giving him credit for being intelligent, she had assumed it was a two-way street.

He saw through her as well.

She had gone on the offensive. Phoning an anonymous tip to an FBI agent.

She had no way of knowing Parks could do nothing against her or any other acting vampire.

He felt helpless.

Arresting her would provoke an avalanche of questions, inquiries, and fail to change anything.

In her life.

His could be marred forever.

"My feline, Carousel, is not here. She is with that cat whisperer. The one who thinks she can talk to cats."

Raize flushed invisibly.

He wanted to grab Amy's arms, put on the metal bracelets, and spin her around until that bright white neck was bent over in a patrol car…

"I came to talk to you." He heard his own voice from a distance. Its crisp deep tone brought him back to the situation emotionally as well as physically.

He regained control.

"You are the registered manager of The Men Unadorned Club."

"What has that got to do with my cat?"

"Nothing. We have a separate investigation going that has

brought the club to our attention. Are you one of the owners?"

Amy took a deep breath.

She knew that ownership of corporations was shielded under a privacy ruling by the Supreme Court. She was under no obligation to answer.

"If you are investigating, and there is any credence to your suspicions, then you should be able to get a warrant."

Raize flushed again.

Three judges had denied such a request.

He was not about to tell Amy.

"It's in the works. I was just hoping you might make my job easier."

"Considering what you cops are paid these days, you need to work harder." Defiant, Amy folded her arms.

"Miss Raxel, don't antagonize me. You don't want me for an enemy."

"I don't want any enemies, Captain."

That statement sounded sincere.

"Then be reasonable, answer my question."

Amy sighed. "Why should I protect anyone? No, I am only a manager."

"Do you know Lars Holt?"

"Yes, he's our regular deliverer."

"How well do you know him?"

"Not well. He's above my social status. Listen, I'm just the manager. All I do is organize entertainment."

"So who does own the club?"

"I don't know." Amy fidgeted as she answered.

"What are the time travel arrangements?"

"The club only caters to private clients. Extra rich people who can afford the best, desiring exotic experiences not provided by legitimate travel sites."

"That makes sense. Legal time travel entertainment is beyond the financial scope of the ordinary person. And there is a long waiting list due to approval requirements and red tape."

"So the rich circumvent regulations. So what? I don't have

anything to do with that aspect of the business. I just send those clients to an address."

"What address?" Raize demanded.

"It changes every time. So that would do you no good." Amy looked out her front window and wished she could time travel right now. "They communicate through the postal system. I get checks for the employees by mail and all my instructions come that way. The owners desire absolute privacy. Whether they get it or not, I don't care. But I cannot help you identify them."

Raize did not believe this story.

But he knew even a court order might not reveal who owned the club. The real names could be buried under many pseudonyms in an elaborate corporate structure.

Protected by the Supreme Court ruling in 2070, ownership of corporations was a privacy right under the Constitution. Made vulnerable only by criminal activity.

It might take dozens of warrants issued individually by a plethora of judges to get at the true owners.

He missed the days of public computer records.

His only hope of gleaning any information was that Electra might bend the rules and search.

He had not much hope of that.

He decided he would do best to rely on old fashioned interview skills.

"I've heard rumors that some people in French Dixie costumes were seen in the club."

He hoped this remark was adequately vague so as not to alert her that a spy was embedded in with her employees.

"That's ridiculous. We would refuse to serve anyone who showed up in such attire. They would be turned away at the door."

Amy's reply had been too quick and her voice a little too breathless for the answer not to have been a rehearsed response.

His interview skills had failed.

He decided Amy Raxel would not help him any further.

"Just sign this consent for me to talk, uh, confer-" He cleared his throat. "Uh, to do whatever I need with your cat."

"No problem."

Amy scrawled a terse signature on the consent form to interview Carousel.

Raize stared at it for a moment, put it in his pocket, bid goodbye to Amy Raxel, and began the drive to Debriah's house.

Anticipating seeing her, not the cat.

Chapter 19

"I'm strapped to a bed. There's no sheets or blankets or quilts. No bedspread. Just the mattress. And I'm naked."

Loyce Landers was speaking into the chip implanted into his wrist, given to him against the rules by Raize Parks. Loyce was now utilizing it to document his captivity in hopes that the coroner would discover it if he did not survive.

"I am not, I repeat, not exercising my Death Option as a police officer. I am being held against my will and any violence done to my person will be against my wishes."

Emboldened by his initial success at infiltrating the secret section of The Men Unadorned Club, Loyce had gone through the china cabinet a second time.

He had put the success of his initial excursion down to his skill and charm, not just pure luck.

He was wrong.

It had been luck.

This time goon-like soldier-costumed men immediately waylaid him at the behest of apparently the same woman who had originally befriended him.

She directed the scene with confusing animosity considering the successful rehearsal they had experienced the first time.

She seemed to project two diverse personalities. And this persona did not like him at all.

He had offered her another rehearsal and she had struck him.

Painfully.

Still reeling from the effects of that blow, he had been tied to the bed in such a way that if he attempted to free himself another painful experience would ensue.

Before leaving him alone, the woman had taken a huge hypodermic needle and injected a cold substance into his arm.

After minutes of paralyzing terror, Loyce remembered the recording chip, fortunately in the other arm.

Loyce stopped talking as he heard the door open. He did not want his captors to discover the device and cut it out of him.

"Are you talking to yourself?"

The voice was sarcastic. Wearing a French Dixie costume with a billowy hat, the woman was almost fully in disguise.

As he tried to focus on her face, hidden under a large floppy had, his vision began to blur.

Another similarly adorned woman was with her. This person was equally illusive in appearance.

The women seemed to be bickering about him.

Yet the voices chimed almost identical save for mild differences in inflection…

"I told you that you were to look for a completely shaven specimen. Couldn't you see this one had long blond hair?"

"I thought I had the right one. He's the one I rehearsed with."

"These performers are not interchangeable."

"You're telling me. This one is enchanting."

"Well, enchanting or not. He's some kind of spy. He's been watching me and observing time travel clients when they arrive."

"Good thing the client never showed up."

"Right. That was a break for us. Give me a few hours alone with him. I'll soon get wind of what he is up to."

Loyce was seeing double and hearing echoes. He wondered vaguely whether there existed two women in reality or just one playing two parts.

Do they know I am a policeman or did I just stumble in at the wrong time and place?

He vaguely surmised the latter was the case.

"He is probably hearing voices by now. You, are you hearing voices?"

Loyce did not reply.

Despite his police training, he was rather surprised these two older women actually would plan to harm him. He was used to much different reactions from older women and those experiences had rendered him somewhat naïve, giving him a blind spot.

"Did you envision that we brought you here to mother you?" asked one of them sarcastically.

"Is this the role-play? How am I doing?" Loyce bluffed, but

with genuine deflation.

"Have you given him the drug?" One addressed the other.

"Yes, it did not take effect at once."

"He's got belly fat."

Unconsciously Loyce began rubbing his abdomen.

The sensation of alarm was so mild. He shook it off.

Habit of my training, he thought.

"Now for your second injection," said the second woman.

A mental red flag popped at the tone of her voice.

He started to sit back up.

In minutes both of the women were on him, one grabbing his arms and the other his legs.

At first, they ignored his exterior.

"Hold him still," she directed the other.

When Loyce saw the size of the syringe she was holding, he became still of his own volition.

He did not want that breaking off inside his arm.

He saw his arm was not the destination.

As they held him down, the taller woman pushed his exterior out of the way and punctured his lower abdomen with the hypodermic needle, which she carefully kept horizontal, just below the skin.

He groggily scanned the women's faces. They were eerily similar and eerily similar to someone else he had seen.

He felt the liquid from the needle spread directly under his exposed flesh, causing the skin directly above to feel cold.

"There that should do it," she said.

The sarcasm in her voice was barely perceptible.

Preoccupied with his predicament, Loyce missed it.

His exterior was now not only fully exposed, but also partially erect.

Athletic, highly trained, used to being able to handle himself in any adversity, Loyce felt little fear at first. He used his strong will to put the all impressions aside and try to reason what to do. Obviously this was an attempt on his life.

But why not just kill him?

Why take any chance on leaving him alive to testify against them?

He strove to structure events sequentially in his brain.

The second woman struck him in his swollen belly.

The astonishment at the woman's action blurred his observation but he tried to recall clearly just what had transpired.

He relived the trauma when the needle had entered his flesh. He recollected a vague unfamiliar pain where the needle had gone in. Now that was gone. Replaced by the sensation of the cold liquid spreading under his skin.

A tingling seemed to flow downward.

This liquid has to be a strong poison, he deduced, temporarily without emotion.

Loyce moaned as his muscles stiffened. It was hard to push air down to his abdomen, but that was the only way he could keep breathing.

He passed out briefly but was soon alert again.

He felt like a large rock was pinning him down and only deep breaths could push it away.

"I was hoping to get another chance at him." One of the women was on him.

"Hurry up," said the other. "I wish you could keep your focus on business."

"It won't wear off for several hours. I'm going to take my time," said the other. "Besides, the client may show up. What will we do then?"

"Don't worry about it."

"I don't suppose he'll be able to give us away after a few hours of this."

Hours of torture, he thought. *But I can take it.*

"Forget about the client."

"So then what happens after we've finished? Are you going to let him go?"

"If he turns out to be spy, we kill him and they will conclude he exercised his Death Option due to the shame."

Distracted by her words, Loyce broke into a sweat that seemed to paralyze any movement, leaving him more rigid.

The woman proceeded with her strategy.

It was not long before he no longer cared what their final plans involved.

If only this torture could last forever.

Chapter 20

Samantha had an emergency request for a counseling session the next day.

Amy Raxel was in the outer office waiting to consult Samantha Speer.

There was one ahead of her, stretched out in the office coffin.

Amy did not mind. She positioned her wall listening device at the correct angle and eavesdropped.

"I sunburn easily. I prefer rare beef."

As her client detailed symptoms, Samantha compiled a list. The young veiled girl was too nervous to speak to with detailed advice. Samantha just wanted to be able to remember all the client revealed when the need for deep counseling arrived.

In case that need arose.

Samantha seriously doubted this client qualified for intensive treatment. She resolved almost at once to counteract the client's unproductive ideas.

"I secretly collect knives."

"Are those your only symptoms?"

"Yes, and it is imperative that I remain anonymous."

Unaware she was being overheard, the girl revealed she had fled her base school and was unlawfully skipping class to keep this appointment.

"Yes, the law allows anonymity in this situation."

"Those are not all my symptoms. I thrill to scare people."

"Have you any fears yourself?"

"My mother will thoroughly reject me. And she is rather a scary person herself."

"Your symptoms are common. Those are hardly enough to go on. Vampirism is much more complicated than that."

"I prefer going out at night. I like to stay indoors. Bright lights hurt my eyes."

"I'm sorry. That is not enough. You are not a candidate for vampire consolation. Perhaps you need to see a mood disorder counselor."

"I just know I'm a vampire! Look at my teeth."

The client bared her pointed teeth. Both canines distinctly came to a point.

"Yes. I see." Samantha hesitated.

A competent dentist easily dealt with that required symptom of vampirism. On the other hand, it was easily faked for those who exulted in the ostracized culture.

"They are genuine. I was born with them. I can prove it."

"That only means you may have latent vampire tendencies. What I mean is, that only means you might be a vampire."

"I have refused several times to have them rounded. Six dentists have reported me. I have the files."

"I see."

"And there is one other thing."

"Yes?"

"During sex my teeth come out."

"What?" Samantha scrutinized the young girl's mouth. "Your teeth look permanent."

"No, I mean, it is an expression. Nouveau, I think, you know for the desire to bite during sex."

"Oh." *These vampire lovers change their terminology like I change clothes,* she thought with contempt. But she spoke professionally. "Well. That's different. Drawing blood?"

"No-o. Well, not yet. I, I don't know why. I just don't want to."

"Have you ever consumed any blood, animal or human, outside of eating rare steaks? You realize that rare steaks are only banned in restaurants. You can eat them at home providing you prepare them yourself."

"I know."

"How often do you eat steak?"

"Almost every day."

"Mmm, hmm."

"So I am a vampire?"

"I did not say that. And make an appointment to see me again next month. Meanwhile, curb your tendencies. Register as a knife collector. Being honest about your hobby will cause you to be accepted as yourself, not suspected as a vampirist. Consider rounding your teeth. Do it yourself with a metal file if you don't like dentists. Stop biting."

"But I don't want to stop. And I'm proud of my pointed teeth. I'm only here because the last dentist threatened if I did not either get help or let him round my teeth, he would have me arrested."

"Dentists cannot have people arrested. Yet. He can only file a complaint. And believe me there are few judges who will only go by a dental report. Police don't even pay attention to dental complainants, they have so many."

"Then I am safe."

"I did not say that either. The law says practicing vampirism in any form is illegal. It does not address the idea of being a vampire. Only the practice of vampire activities."

"I don't understand."

"I shouldn't say this. But assuming no one is reporting anything you do except the dentists who target your pointed teeth, you will not encounter legal problems. But if you publicly declare, well, that is consequential. Don't ask. Don't tell"

"A BAD policy, in my opinion. So what about the sunburns?"

"Stop staying out in the sun too long."

The client sighed. "I suppose you are right."

"Listen, you are young, with your whole life ahead of you. Don't embrace vampirism without investigating all the facts. Set another date with me for next month and follow my advice in the meantime. Let me ask you this. Any new person in your life recently?"

"Yes. Well, I have my eye on someone. A red haired man. An athlete."

"Is that the real reason you are here."

"Suppose I bit him in the heat of passion?"

"We can work on ways to curb that urge."

"Okay."

"Try not to worry. Trust me. You will be fine."

Chapter 21

While waiting, Amy Raxel continued listening to all this with her illegal listener. It was a device disguised as a costume jewelry brooch and amplified sound through ordinary sheetrock walls.

She did not want to tell any true details of her life so she had arrived early to try to get ideas of what to say.

She wished she could see.

However, she had no wall viewer and she had failed to glimpse the girl's face, catching only a familiar outline as the client entered the private office with Samantha.

She suspected the unidentified girl might be someone she knew. However, she could not be sure.

The counselee could be anyone.

The recorder masked the true nature of the voices but Amy did feel sure this was a young person.

Samantha Speer's comments confirmed this.

So Amy prepared to modify her narrative to make it fit her age.

Clients entered Samantha Speer's home office through one door and exited through another so the room was empty when Amy Raxel was allowed in.

Fortunately before Samantha returned, Amy remembered to remove the false caps on her pointed teeth. Somewhat rattled by that near oversight, Amy presented the classic demeanor of a nervous initial visit patient, who had called for an emergency consultation late in the afternoon.

With only minor modifications, she mimicked the previous client's concerns, seeking to get the same advice.

Samantha's counseling was almost word for word, save for the speech about being young.

Amy noticed its absence with some bitterness but overall she was satisfied.

Amy was unsure why Raize Parks had ignored all the obvious signs and not arrested her after their interview.

She did not want to take any chances.

Just consulting with a vampire consoler would put her on record as being penitent, enough evidence to prove she had sought help if Raize Parks called her out on vampirism.

Like in days gone by when drugs were illegal, a willingness to undergo rehab kept perpetrators out of jail.

She would offer her consultation with Samantha as proof that she was resisting any criminal activity. Practices such as venturing into the dark underground of the vampire world and attending a vampire support group.

She did so without misgivings.

Her excursions there were few and far between because each experience satisfied her for a long period of time and it was safer and cheaper to venture into that culture only when desire demanded it

Like the previous unknown client, she made an appointment for next week.

However, she intended to reschedule ad infinitum.

Samantha walked with her client to the bus stop, watched Amy get on, and meandered back home.

"People like that woman at first, then soon forget they ever met her, Samantha concluded with automatic analysis.

This had been her last patron for the day. She was afraid to face the evening alone.

She consciously dismissed Amy from her mind simultaneously passing beyond threshold of her front door.

Yet subconsciously her mind initiated a trajectory of comparison leading to a mental venture into her past.

Samantha had never considered herself attractive.

At fifteen, she fell in love with a vampire who was interested in only a vampire relationship. Brokenhearted, she blamed herself.

The horror of a subsequent unsuccessful encounter or a vampiristic experience kept her from interacting frequently with the opposite sex.

As a result she had fantasized about doomed relationships ever since.

The chance meeting with Loyce was a fairytale come true for

her.

Now she beheld it evaporating into thin air, obliterating any reason for drawing any bright future images.

He had not contacted her except for a couple of do-not-reply texts.

With no explanation for his inaccessibility, her anticipation turned to ongoing anxiety.

She had risked an Internet search but found no results indicating he ever existed.

She dialed Debriah.

Debriah had almost not answered the phone. She was expecting a dramatic evening herself.

However, she saw who the caller was and responded.

Samantha poured out her worst fears in a torrent of frantic words.

"So you cannot locate Loyce yet?" Succinctly summing up, Debriah's tone did mirror Samantha's concern, causing an increase in the latter's blood pressure.

"You think something terrible has happened?"

"He might have duties and concerns that take him away from his everyday life."

"Don't try to reassure me. I know he should have contacted me by now."

"Listen, I will consult Captain Parks." Debriah did not reveal she expected Raize to arrive at any minute.

"Oh, would you? I know you are in contact with him about the cat witnessing the murders."

"Right. And I will bring up Loyce Smith to him. Perhaps he can find out something. But, Samantha, you have to be realistic. These love at first sight romances rarely work out in the long run."

"Is that a psychic prediction?"

Debriah was surprised at the hostility in Samantha's voice.

"No, no. Not at all. I have had no revelations concerning anybody recently. Please, I'm just trying to help."

Samantha apologized.

The doorbell sounded.

"Let me go so I can call the Captain. I think he may be working late today."

A singsong sound went off and Samantha looked at her secret smartphone, the one illicit item she had bought on the black market.

It had an unlawful chip that made it functional, albeit unreliable. It was prone to revert to Chinese and she had to reprogram it in English frequently.

Today she saw only a request for a return call on the number she gave only to her clients in case they needed to talk with her anonymously.

She hit redial.

"Hello?" she spoke cautiously.

"I'm calling as a friend," said an obviously disguised voice. "I know you are a vampire consoler and you have a friend named Debriah Brock."

"Yes, are you calling to suggest Debriah Brock is a vampire? If so you're ridiculous-"

"No, you don't understand. I want to report a vampire. But not your friend. I know you are actually an anti-vampirist activist who has become a vampire consoler in order to counsel those who assume they are vampires into a different conclusion and to identify those who really are vampires so you can turn them in."

"What gives you the right to say that to me? I am an ethical professional. Tolerant and nonjudgmental."

"Don't bother. I know the truth. I don't care that you are an informant to the anti-vampire movement. I'm on your side. I want the vampires eliminated also."

Samantha calmed down.

"So what are you saying?"

"Your friend's friend is a vampire. Raize Parks."

The caller hung up, leaving Samantha unnerved again and staring at the blank screen of the phone.

The caller obviously did not know the number was private to such a few people.

Or made to a smartphone that could trace the location of the caller.

96

Samantha did not think twice. She began at once accessing the illegal South American Internet…

Across town, unaware she was being tracked, Amy Raxel folded her arms with satisfaction.

It had been an impulsive act of offense but Amy had no doubt she was wise in making the first move.

If he came for her and the legal defense did not work for her, she would bring Raize Parks down the hard way.

Blackmail. Exposure. Ruination…

Even death…

Chapter 22

"I would like to nibble at your neck," Raize whispered to Debriah.

They were at her house.

In her bed.

Totally without clothing.

Debriah twisted her shoulders. "Go ahead. Carousel doesn't care."

Raize glared at the cat in his peripheral vision. She was grooming herself inconspicuously.

He had forgotten she was present.

He decided to ignore her.

"Go ahead," Debriah repeated. Her eyes closed.

"I might hurt you."

Debriah quelled exasperation.

She ached for him so.

She wanted his lips on her neck.

She did not care if he hurt her. She did not care if he killed her.

She opened her eyes and studied his face.

He looked stressed.

He was.

Debriah had no way of knowing his vampire tendencies tended to come out during sex and this was the reason he had curtailed his sexual activities since beginning his career.

A long time. "Tell me about your first time," Raize said evenly.

"I actually first made love when I was 17," Debriah murmured almost modestly. "He was a wonderful man but he had a Death Option he could not resist."

Why did all men want to know about their predecessors? What difference does it make to them?

Raize put his hands over her ears and caressed her forehead with his lips. She felt a tiny bit of skin above her eyebrow being scraped by his teeth.

Gently scraped.

Chills went down her spine.

"A young boy with a Death Option?" Regardless of what he was doing, Raize's mind was still on her past sex life.

The cop in him is ever inquisitive.

"No, uh, he was older. He was your age."

Raize took a step away from her.

"I did not get him killed," said Debriah defensively. "No one ever knew about us. He was a soldier. He took a Death Option."

"I see."

"Raize, there has not been anyone for me seriously since him."

"So am I similar to him?"

"No. Not really. He was impulsive, quick tempered, and volatile. And also- married."

"But you loved him?"

"Yes. Ten years ago. Now I think- I know I am falling in love with you."

"Another secret affair? You would be happy with that?"

Raize felt inwardly glad any relationship with Debriah was forbidden and must remain secret because that would keep her from talking about him.

Theoretically.

"At least you're not married. Surely we could apply for permits."

"I cannot risk it. Not with my past. I have a record that I must keep classified or I will lose my job."

"How do you explain it to people who gain access to classified information?"

"I say I was undercover."

"Why don't we just make love in the normal way? And you can keep saying that."

"That would still be illegal. It is not the way we do it but our age difference."

"No one would ever know if you don't want them to."

"You don't fully realize my position. Not only would I be risking my career, I could go to jail. My past could be exposed as real, not just a cover story. How do you envision I would fare in that situation? What options would I have?"

"Not the Death Option? Surely you have more sense than that."

Debriah pulled him near to her protectively.

"No, I- well, for personal reasons I don't consider the Death Option open to me."

"Then I will apply for an age variance. I can be older."

"You'd be turned down. You look too young to get an age variance. In addition, you would lose so many years of accumulated benefits. I could not let you do it."

"Then I could have myself aged medically."

"Absolutely not! I forbid it!"

Despite the gravity of their situation, a rush of joy overwhelmed Debriah.

He really loves me, she exulted. *Or he would not care so much.*

Debriah listened only halfway to Raize's lecture on the evils of medical aging. How dangerous it was, how unattractive it made the patients, how useless in the end.

In the middle of this opine, a sound rang loud and clear.

"Meow!"

Carousel was hungry.

Raize dropped the subject of medical aging. "I know you can talk to her- hey don't get mad- I might can accept that she can talk to you but what about me?"

"Huh?"

Debriah went into the kitchen. Raize followed.

The can opener whirred as it opened a large can of tuna.

"When I'm speaking, can she understand me? Can all cats or other animals understand the people conversing around them?"

"They tell me mostly no." Debriah spooned the tuna in a large bowl. "Mayonnaise?"

Carousel shook her tail.

She meowed.

"I assume that meant no?" Raize asked.

I actually take tuna plain, Carousel wanted to say, but it was not important enough to summon the necessary energy to speak directly to Debriah.

"I didn't know. Sorry it's in oil."

That's okay this time, thought Carousel as she dived into the bowl...

Debriah petted her lovingly as she ate.

Raize cleared his throat. "Um- person trying to communicate here. Remember? Sex? Love? Etc. Although watching you feed the cat in the nude is quite interesting."

"Oh, sorry. As I was saying, apparently they can hear other people who are not whisperers but it's like hearing a foreign language. However, like two people who don't speak the same language and live together, ultimately they can translate some if they try hard enough."

"The same could be said for cops and criminals," said Raize not without sincerity.

"By the way." She changed the subject with a light voice. "A friend of mine is worried about her new boyfriend."

"Is he involved in medical aging? Or stepping out with an unauthorized prospect."

"No. Just forget that. He's not doing anything wrong. He's just disappeared on her."

"So? Under what circumstances? Has she reported him missing?"

"That's just it. She cannot ascertain any evidence he exists. But she was practically ready to marry him until he vanished."

As they walked back to the bedroom, Debriah briefly described Samantha and Loyce's love affair, initially without mentioning names.

"Perhaps he sought to fade away. The Men Unadorned Club is under suspicion for deliberate disappearances right now. Relationship moving too fast? Or likely he was married."

"Maybe. But I promised her I would mention him to you. He sounded so promising. He swore to her that he had a degree in linguistics and spoke several languages. He comes from a large family with several brothers and sisters. He wants to marry her and sire children. And they match perfectly in every way. Or so it seemed. Nothing like that ever happened to her before. She's frantic. Could you poke around and get some information about him?"

"Okay. What's his name?"

Raize gave no indication that the name Loyce Smith meant anything to him.

Debriah noticed he grew tenser but she assumed his mood worsened because he was comparing Samantha and Loyce's socially approved relationship with their own status.

"I'm sure it is nothing. The boy probably got cold feet. Tell your friend there is a 98 percent chance he is okay."

"I told her I would ask you to look into it."

"Without being able to tell you anything, let me assure you he is safe."

"Seriously?"

"Yes, but you did not hear it from me."

"Okay. But please get him to get in touch with Samantha."

"I cannot do that. I can't tell you anything other than he is safe."

They had become distracted by their conversation and were lounging casually on either side of the bed.

Words were causing too much distance.

Eager to resume touching him, Debriah did not press her request.

"I want you, Raize," she said simply. "Any way we can get away with it."

"There is no legal path for us," he summed up.

But he put his hands on her hips and pressed her against him.

Lost in the wonders of love, she did not reply.

"We have to have a superb cover story."

"Now I have an idea."

Raize listened with admiration at the simplicity of Debriah's suggestion.

"Why not? If anybody looks into where I was, that will prove I was not here."

"Have you ever actually done that? Rented a bed at the

library?"

"No, but I did register as a reader."

"As a what?"

"I can volunteer to read to hospital patients. If you set up a pattern of renting a library bed and I volunteer, it could be a means of meeting if circumstances warrant."

"True. And registering for the night for a bed would give me a cover for spending the night with you."

"Sound good?"

"Probably the best we can do. Society makes our love against the law. I need your assurance you realize the consequences and are willing to take the risk," he finished.

Debriah still did not reply.

"Debriah? Did you hear me?"

"Oh, everything about us is illegal!"

She pushed him down unexpectedly on the bed and pulled. Stunned, his reflexive defensive mode failed.

"If you won't bite my neck, I'll bite yours."

And her teeth came out.

Chapter 23

Electra insisted Raize meet her at his office Saturday morning.

Raize wanted to convince Electra the vanishings of Lars Holt and Magdalene Rene Watters were as serious as the disappearances connected to The Men Unadorned Club.

He did not want to tell her that he had concluded that Lars Holt and Magdalene Rene Watters were the two people the cat had seen slain.

He did not want to tell her he believed a cat.

He did not want to reveal anything about Debriah Brock.

He did not yet want to tell her about Loyce Landers.

He was amused at hearing Loyce had fallen in love on the job. Raize figured Loyce had plausible reason not to contact his new love interest so was not worried that the new sweetheart had not heard from him.

Loyce Landers could be counted on to do his job at any cost. The impetuousness of the relationship did not surprise the police captain.

Raize had observed that Loyce routinely claimed whatever he sought when he encountered it.

Loyce's aggressive nature, combined with a friendly personable attitude, yielded vital elements of his suitability for undercover work.

Devotion to the rule of law and practical priorities completed the needed personality mix.

Electra, on the other hand, needed concrete scenarios in order to function. She never went undercover.

Raize continued explaining.

"We have two missing persons. We have a cat whisperer reporting a cat witnessed two people being killed and they fit the description of the missing persons. That is what I have reported. How can your superior claim there is not a connection?"

Raize gazed impatiently at Electra. He felt more irritated with his colleague than usual.

Images of Debriah Brock played on his mind.

"Two supposedly dead people who have no known connection to each other?" Electra's voice was almost scornful.

"Not true. Lars Holt was the routine deliverer for The Men Unadorned Club. Amy Raxel, the very efficient manager of the club owns the cat. That's a coincidence too much for me. Plus she lives not too far from the Holt family residence. I would not be surprised to learn they are both connected to the club owners."

"I haven't been able to uncover who owns the club."

This truly surprised Raize. She might frequently disagree with his conclusions, be overly loyal to her superior, but Electra normally exuded extraordinary efficiency.

She complicated this unofficial conference by going off on the wrong track.

"What about this cat whisperer? I consider her a viable suspect."

"Suspect for what?" Raize's blood pressure rose.

"Well, kidnapping and or murder. Assuming what you surmise is true. Fact is many times the person reporting a crime is actually the perpetrator."

"I don't think so. I am confident she was doing her duty in reporting what the cat told her."

"You don't actually think she can talk to cats."

"I'm paid to follow up leads from the public, no matter what species they come from."

"All that scientific crap about talking to animals is no more believable than the life after death proposition. I don't hold with any of that."

"No?"

"And I don't think you do either. You're too smart. Is it that you just want to see that young and beautiful cat whisperer?"

Two notions crossed Raize's mind at that instant.

Has she been checking upon me?

Why would she designate Debriah Brock as beautiful?

Raize Parks did not see people in terms of appearance, rather how they made him feel. He began to analyze his visual memories of Debriah.

"Did you interview the widow?" Electra interrupted his analysis of Debriah's features.

Maybe she is beautiful, he realized with some surprise.

"Did you talk to the widow?" Electra repeated. "What did she say?"

"No. She filed a report. I spoke to her on the phone. Nothing apparent there. She does not know. I'll write a report about my interview with her tomorrow."

Electra sighed. "Want to go for a drink tonight? Maybe you can fill me in then. Then you won't be required to write a report."

"No, I have to work late," he said abruptly.

He got up and secured his firearm in preparation to leave. He exited the room without a further farewell.

Electra stared at him for a few moments prior to making a hasty exit from his office.

In any other circumstances, she would have told Raize that Lars Holt's widow was a regular at The Men Unadorned Club.

Electra knew Raize would eventually discover Marlotta Holt's entertainment habits.

However, her just being a patron of such a place was not enough to draw any concrete conclusions.

Electra wondered what other facts Raize might have detected. Facts she could no longer count on him sharing with her.

She wanted to get ahead of him.

A plan was already forming.

It was so hard to believe he was a vampire.

She had found no such tendencies in Debriah Brock. Formerly registered as a psychic but she had renounced that unseemly but lucrative profession esteemed in only anti-establishment circles. In addition, an only child, estranged from her much older parents who lived nearby.

Why they were estranged, Electra could not ascertain.

Probably because she went from being a psychic to being a cat whisperer, a notable decline socially and economically. Her parents were disappointed.

What did Raize see in her?

Electra put no stock in the idea that the cat whisperer actually possessed any information about the missing people.

She was anxious about the important missing deliverer, Lars Holt. However, she felt there probably existed a reasonable explanation for his stepping out of sight for a while.

Men like Lars Holt, men like Raize Parks, frequently craved solitude, respite from their demanding professions.

Electra could have allowed for Raize taking as much time as he ever needed unless she discovered another female in his life.

Feeling rejected, she slumped in her car until he walked out the door, a short time later.

"Just wanted to get me out of the way," she muttered as she started her engine, intending to follow him.

She shrank inwardly, already bone tired. And craving sugar.

She wished for the camera, still authorized for her but banned for most others.

She did not have it with her this night.

For fear of blowing her cover, Electra rarely carried it

With it, she could have documented the kiss Raize Parks greeted Debriah with when they met at the library.

Using a public facility to further their illegal activities!

Electra pulled a candy bar from her purse and ate it.

The idea that she had lost Raize to a criminal relationship with a younger woman- a relationship she did not dare openly report without revealing her own unethical behavior- not against the law but enough to get her fired- infuriated the agent.

If she could use vampirsm against him she would, but this collusion with a much younger woman offered an even better way to gain control over him.

He could excuse vampirsm as undercover work or get treatment for it and renounce it.

Loving a younger woman was inexcusable. Highly illegal under any circumstances.

The candy bar eased her anger.

A warm glow enveloped Electra, igniting a little energy.

The plan jelled.

She had him now.

He is going to marry me whether he wants to or not, she decided.

Then I'll never let him out of my sight.

Chapter 24

Shortly after Electra summoned Raize to work, Debriah's landline rang.

Samantha, still worried about Loyce after not hearing from him for over three days, reached out to Debriah, again by phone.

"So you cannot locate Loyce? After this much time?"

Debriah's tone mirrored Samantha's concern, causing an increase in the latter's blood pressure.

"He does not respond to any way I try to contact him."

Debriah curbed her impulse to lecture Samantha about forbidden communication devices.

She knew her friend had no qualms about purchasing merchandise on the black market.

Debriah could do nothing about it at the present time.

Maybe someday.

Judge not and ye be not judged, Debriah reminded herself sternly.

"I'm sure he is okay."

"I cannot lose him. Not now that I've found him! He's so exceptional. So extremely attractive."

That's the way I feel about Raize, thought Debriah. *But I will have to keep my love a secret.*

Extreme envy overwhelmed her.

Just for a moment.

"We have to do something! Can't you explore unexplained absences with your psychic ability?"

"No. It's not that simple. You need to relax. Check out a good book to read. Something like *How to Tell Whether Your Lover has Left You.*"

"He had not left me! He's very devoted. He wants to marry me. He loves me terribly. He'd do anything for me. He's in terrible trouble. I just know it!"

"There's nothing I can do about this."

"You promised me you'd get your police lover to help."

"I never committed to-"

"From what all you have told me about him, I suspect him."

"Suspect him? He is the law!"

"I think he is a vampire!"

"Samantha! You see vampires coming out of every closet."

"I know my duty in this world. And it is to expose vampires. I console those who come to me for counseling, deluded that they are vampires. But those actively practicing the vampirist occult, I turn them in."

Debriah frowned. She had been previously vague about Samantha's latter role.

"I thought you were trying to help vampires."

"Vampires cannot be helped. True vampires never change. They will return to their behavior no matter how much counseling or supposed rehabilitation they receive."

"Samantha, I assure you. Raize Parks is not a vampire. Loyce is perfectly safe. Take my word for it."

"Oh, so you did tell him. What's going on?"

"I cannot tell you. Only Loyce may not be what he seems."

"Is he really a cop? Is he a vampire?"

"You are letting your imagination run away. Now stop worrying. Raize assures me that your friend is safe."

"Raize Parks has vampire tendencies I just know it!"

"Maybe there's a little vampirism in all of us."

"Oh, Debriah. You don't comprehend what you are saying. Vampires are evil, responsible for more grief in this world than politicians."

"You are prejudiced, Samantha."

"Debriah, just ask him if he fears being stabbed through the heart with a silver dagger. See what he says."

"Samantha, everybody would say yes."

"I'm just trying to warn you. But I'm not going to lecture you. I'm too worried about Loyce."

"I completely trust Raize. He stated he would check into it. He did. And Loyce is perfectly safe. I'm positive about that!"

Debriah's assurances slowed Samantha's pessimism but she continued to view Loyce's absence as ominous.

Samantha and Debriah spent Saturday afternoon without contact from their new lovers.

Loyce remained unreachable.

Debriah did not hear from Raize. While this did not concern her due to the nature of his work, it did little to help Samantha, who persisted in calling Debriah again early evening. Her voice over the phone sounded more stressed than ever.

"I don't care what your lover says. It's three days since I have heard from mine. And nothing but a couple of texts for a week. Texts with 'no reply' requested. I'm worried to death."

Debriah gave in. "Can you meet me in the parking lot?"

"So you do think he is still there? Why? Has Raize Parks told you something?"

Samantha's anxiety boiled over.

"I cannot betray confidences. Just maybe he's there but just not taking any calls."

This used to be a place I could come and just relax and forget all about vampires, Samantha recalled with regret as she and Debriah entered the club. *I'll never be able to thoroughly enjoy that atmosphere again. All that is left will be libraries…*

She was a little jealous as Debriah perked up at the sight of the performers.

"Remember why we are here." She poked Debriah's arm.

"Oh, yes indeed." Debriah pulled her eyes away from the tall redheaded gymnast with a neatly trimmed pointed beard.

She took a deep breath.

Samantha grabbed the athlete by the arm.

"We need to see the manager."

"Have I done something wrong?"

"No, not at all. Nothing to do with you. We seek some information."

Samantha waved a bill in front of the performer.

"She's that person right over there." He pointed and snatched the money from Samantha's hand. "But she's just an employee like us. She doesn't know anything."

111

He danced off as the women regarded the frizzy haired manager standing near an empty table, scrutinizing a menu.

"I think that is Amy Raxel, Carousel's owner," Debriah said.

"I know her also. Under different circumstances."

"Then let's corner her and make her take us to the real powers on the premises."

"So you think she knows who owns this place?"

"No, Raize said the same thing as that dancer. She's just the manager. Only an employee. He had not been able to identify the owner yet."

"She has to know who the real power here is. Let's demand to a face-to-face with the proprietor. Blackmail Amy Raxel if we have to," declared Samantha. "I can get this woman to talk."

It was hard for Debriah to tell who acted more astonished to see the other- Amy or Samantha.

Swiftly, Samantha achieved the upper hand without speaking a word. Facial expression was more powerful.

Striving to maintain a calm demeanor, Amy melted inside.

Chapter 25

"So you are in need of a break. Our exotic time travel experience is just the cure for stress."

So opined the brochure in the inner office where Amy Raxel had her private desk.

Non-verbal persuasion, accompanied by a formal request to see Loyce, got them beyond the outer time travel sales office.

Debriah and Samantha had been covertly led through a door labeled 'closet' into a hall through another door into a small room.

"The performers live here if they desire and we monitor their bedrooms via a closed circuit system. "You can see your friend's bed is empty."

The manager perched on an elevated platform with real time onscreen views of all parts of the club, including the performance area.

"Stop looking at the screen showing the men dancing." Samantha scowled at Debriah.

"Is this legal? I must report this if I see a suspect situation."

"No problem," said Amy smoothly. "Our screens are closed circuit, for viewing only. We make no recordings. The devices have been decommissioned so they only project video. We have waivers for privacy rights from all entertainers. You actually get a better view on the screen than you do in person. You can zoom in and make enlargements. Feast your eyes."

Both visitors stared fixated as Amy zoomed in on the same red haired man Debriah had noticed earlier.

All his hair shined red.

Samantha turned away, remembering how blond Loyce was in that vicinity.

Debriah remained glued to the screen.

Amy handed the remote control to Debriah.

"I know we met earlier but I trust I can rely on your ethical discretion." Amy spoke in a whisper to Samantha as Debriah proceeded to focus strategically on several dancers.

Samantha's desire to locate Loyce and ascertain his safety

113

overwhelmed her professional ethics.

She informed Amy if Loyce was not produced in person or at least an explanation with some kind of proof of what happened to Loyce, and that he was safe, privacy would take a backseat to the vampire consoler's legal obligation to report vampirsm genuinely perceived as a threat.

After protestations and accusations of attempted blackmail failed to move Samantha, Amy capitulated.

She did know at least one owner, she admitted.

And that person was on the premises.

"I'm just the manager. I don't have the authority to get you the answers you need. I'll get one of the owners for you. Then you will understand your ideas that we would harm anyone at the club are way over the top. But you must agree to pose as time travel clients."

"We can do that," said Debriah, still focusing on the dancers.

"If I don't find out where my friend is, I will report you to the authorities as a practicing vampire."

"So much for client confidentiality. I'm going to introduce you as time travel prospects and if you don't play along and follow my lead, I'll see to it you never lay eyes on your friend again." Amy angrily left the room.

"Who does she think she is?" Samantha shut the door behind Amy.

"You could lose your license for this," Debriah whispered at her friend.

"No such thing as client confidentiality. She's breaking the law. She either gets the owner and he tells us where Loyce is or I'm calling the authorities and reporting her as a practicing vampire." Samantha turned her back to Debriah.

"I think we will get more information by playing along. Let's try that first."

They did not have long to wait.

Amy entered first, then another person followed, coming from the inside of the china cabinet.

Samantha gaped at this emergence with her mouth open. Debriah had returned her attention to the screen and missed the entrance.

"I understand you are suffering stress in your life right now." The second person addressed Samantha. "Perhaps we can help."

"I demand to know where one of your dancers is. He has been unreachable for several days."

"He may have gone back in time," said the woman.

"You expect me to believe that?"

"And should I be interested in your personal beliefs, Ms.?"

"Speer, Samantha Speer. I'm an officer of the court."

"May I ask in what capacity?"

"I'm a vampire consoler."

"Indeed?"

Amy cleared her throat. The other woman nodded at her.

"We offer select experiences here that we call time travel. Of course there is no such thing. But it is perfectly innocent. Our clients know what they are signing up for. It's role-play," said Amy.

"I'm the owner," admitted the tall, thin, professionally dressed woman. "One of them anyway. I'm sure I can count on your discretion. Corporate ownership is protected privacy."

"Possibly." Samantha's tone sounded conciliatory but still had an edge of danger.

"Entrepreneurship is a dangerous profession but I am determined anti-capitalists shall never dissuade me from my life's calling. I consider it a scared trust to run a business and The Men Unadorned Club does much good in this bleak world."

"I don't disagree, Ms.-"

"Holt, Marlotta Holt."

Debriah jumped, now partially diverted from the screen of dancing naked men.

She recognized the name as that of the wife of the missing deliverer. She also had the distinct impression she had seen the woman somewhere else. That impression came on fuzzy but strong.

Now I can tell Raize who really owns The Men Unadorned Club, she thought excitedly, recalling this had been a piece of information denied him.

She tried to not show her excitement. The knowledge could be hazardous. As far as Marlotta Holt was concerned, there could be no way she could be aware of Carousel's eyewitness account of the murders at her home or that Debriah was at all involved.

At least, Debriah hoped so.

"I'm here to find out the welfare of my friend, Loyce Smith," Samantha said.

"Oh? So that is what this is? A welfare check?"

"I fear he is in danger. I demand to make contact with him and get reassurances he is not. Or else I want emergency responders here at once."

"There exists no reason for concern. None at all. Amy, would you please leave us. I need to talk to these ladies privately."

"But don't you want me to-"

"Go, Amy. Locate which stage this young man is performing on. Get a viewing set up."

Debriah saw this as a perfect opportunity to exit.

"This is actually just the affair of my friend here. I tagged along with her to lend support. I should go."

"Nonsense," said Marlotta.

"Please don't leave," begged Samantha.

"You two came into this together. You might as well experience the truth together."

"I need you as a witness," Samantha whispered fiercely.

"No need for whispering," said Marlotta. "It is not talk that will solve this question. I am going to show you that Mr., um Smith, is alive and well and show you that he is not in any danger, in fact he is enjoying himself immensely. As I said earlier, we offer a time travel experience. You have heard of time travel?"

Debriah flinched, remembering her all too real disorder. "Yes, I have."

Marlotta, and even Samantha, who knew of her sufferings, missed the sarcasm in her voice.

"Just to save time and trouble I am going to give you two an experience reserved only for our primary investors. Come this way."

Back through the door inside the large china cabinet, Marlotta led them down a long hall and into a theatre where a tall curtain swept across a large stage.

Marlotta seated them in fold down opera seats facing a tall massive curtain.

"Wait right here. I've got to prepare for my scene. You are only going to get sneak peek. So don't plan to catch the entire act for free."

She swept away from them in an exaggerated huff.

Debriah and Samantha gripped the arms of their chairs, facing the curtain in silence.

Amy produced two bags of popcorn and mutely deposited them in cup holders in the arms of the chairs.

She brought Cokes and hotdogs on trays and set them on either side of the two women.

Debriah slowly picked her popcorn up and began to munch.

She sipped her drink and eyed the hotdog.

Samantha glared with hostility so Debriah stuck with the popcorn.

Then the curtain parted.

Chapter 26

"How could he?"

Those words summed up Samantha's feelings in a nutshell.

Almost nothing had been said while the two friends glimpsed the scene between Loyce and Marlotta.

They had exited the room in silence, Debriah carrying her hotdog but Samantha abandoning everything as Amy directed them back out to the performance area in The Men Unadorned Club.

Not even spending any time in the performance area, they had gone straight back to Debriah's house.

The time crept beyond Midnight, now Sunday early hours.

Neither entertained the idea of sleep.

Samantha had spoken no more words than were necessary to request companionship. Then she erupted.

"Loyce was just lying there while she- she pleasured herself on top of him! And that other woman telling them to give it their all because the clients have finally shown up. What did that mean?"

"I don't know. Maybe there's an explanation."

"There could never be an explanation for that. I don't care how much they pay him. He led me on. He claimed he loved me. He- He-."

"It is probably just work to him. The daily grind."

"Ha! And the worst part is I had been planning to call my family and tell them I had found someone at last!"

Samantha's consciousness mourned all the major decisions of her life.

Leaving her parents and two brothers in Wisconsin five years ago to try to seek a better future in Texas where there were more vampires.

Frequenting male stripper clubs the past year and everything in between.

Debriah considered her grieved friend with trepidation. "I'm not sure this is all it appeared to be. You know, there was something familiar about Marlotta Holt in her costume. She reminded me terribly of Carlotta Fortune in *Twilight of the French South*."

"Oh, how can you prattle on about that old movie at a time like this?"

"But she looked just like her. Only older."

"I wish you'd get that obsession out of your mind. I'm glad I never saw that film."

"I tell you she morphed into an older version of Carlotta Fortune."

"Carlotta Fortune is dead."

"But- the names, Marlotta, Carlotta, don't you think that is a coincidence? I think it is quite a coincidence that those names rhyme, don't you agree?"

"No. And I never want to hear either name again! Oh, at least I never told anyone about him but you. How could I face my family in Wisconsin if I had told them? Thank God, I procrastinated taking him to visit them in person. Now he'll never go!"

Samantha burst into tears.

Debriah gently took her friend in hand.

"The best way to handle the bad times in life is to do something for others. This a fine opportunity for you to start your volunteer reading work. You can give hope to others."

Feeling completely helpless, Samantha agreed.

She allowed Debriah to drive her to the library.

The plan had been that Raize would be renting a bed. Debriah figured she could get Samantha settled in for the night and take off with Raize, without her friend being the wiser.

However, after searching all the beds in the cool dimly lighted sleeping section, Debriah could not find Raize.

He was not there.

She had been informed that all the library beds were full for the night, some with more than one occupant.

Provided she wanted to stay around with discretion, and hope Raize showed up, she had no alternative but to actually read aloud to someone.

Samantha signed up to be a reader. She was finishing her application at the front desk as Debriah circled back after her unsuccessful search for Raize.

"I'm not feeling sleepy at all," Samantha was telling the librarian. "My friend and I both need to work off some stress."

The librarian nodded solemnly. "Therapeutic reading saves lives."

"Does it?" Debriah spoke breathlessly, her eyes on Samantha's elbow jerking back and forth as she filled in the form with a ballpoint pen.

"That's the name of our program. Read a Book, Save a Life." She handed Samantha a book with a gracious smile.

"Must be true," whispered Samantha to Debriah.

"Down that corridor to the left is the hospital wing," she said to the visitors. "These are the next books on the list to be read to patients. Just check in with the night nurse."

"I'm already registered." Debriah presented her ID.

The librarian slapped the ID on the counter and slid a book at Debriah without looking up at her.

Samantha and Debriah silently walked the polished floors and entered through the swinging doors to the adjacent hospital complex.

The nurse looked at the books in their hands.

"*Murder as the Organist Plays.* I know that book. It is a thriller about a love affair that went wrong."

"Just what I need," said Samantha.

"Good," said the nurse. "There is a comatose patient in room 112. Begin reading the novel to that person."

"And me?"

"Let's see. You get science fiction. *3748 A.D. The Return of the Cat* by Carl S. Kralich. I've read that one also."

"That's quite a coincidence."

"Actually I've read every book in the library."

"Oh."

"This is light science fiction reading with humor. There's a talking cat in it. Just hilarious. The writer acts like the cat can just talk like us." The librarian laughed. "Pure fiction of course."

Debriah examined the book. "It must have been written in the previous century before scientists revealed that some of us can initiate brain wave connections with cats that allow us to communicate."

The librarian scowled. "You need to go to another corridor, turn right and read to the next name on the list there. An orderly will assist you if you get lost."

Debriah did as instructed but was a little confused when the supposed entry to that corridor actually led outside.

As she was looking around in amazement, the orderly asked whether she needed assistance.

"I am supposed to read to the sick, but this appears to be the cemetery."

"Correct," said the orderly. "We instituted a new program to read to the recently deceased. If they are buried in the library's cemetery we check to see what book they were in the middle of and see to it that the book is finished posthumously."

"I had not heard of that program."

"I notice you got that fictional sci-fi cat book. Take it to that tombstone just erected over there." He pointed. "Chairs are stacked on the lawn. The deceased was on page 52 but you might start at the end of the previous chapter."

"I'm curious." Debriah chatted with the orderly as he assisted her with a chair. "Is this service included in burial in the library's cemetery?"

"No it costs extra. There is an initial fee and monthly renewal."

Wonder who pays the bills?

Debriah settled in and started reading the book.

"Oh you don't have to read aloud if you don't want to. He cannot hear you. Just mentally project the words to the deceased."

Incensed, Debriah lost her place.

"That is not correct. I'll have you know that does not work."

"How would you know?"

Debriah hesitated. She did not want to say she was or had ever been a psychic.

"I'll read aloud, I hope you don't mind."

"Suit yourself."

The orderly placed the chair and left.

"I'm going to file a complaint," Debriah whispered to Samantha when they met back up in the main lobby of the library.

"So you did read out loud in the cemetery?"

"Yes, of course."

"You probably got as much reaction from your listener as I did from mine," said Samantha. "I'm going to check out something to read for myself and rent a bed for the rest night. I don't wish to read about romance or cats. Are you staying the night?"

A few people had checked out early, leaving space available.

"No. I do need to speak with Carousel again. I am going to talk to Raize about all this and he wanted me to ask her again about what she saw. So before I speak to him I'm going to do what he asked."

"Please don't tell him about Loyce and that woman!"

"I won't mention Loyce's name. But I have got to let Raize know what goes on at that club."

"Promise me you won't mention Loyce."

"I promise. You'll feel better after you rest here. I'll get my session with Carousel over with, then catch up on my sleep in my own bed."

Back home alone with the feline, Debriah positioned the cat on the sofa and endeavored to make her own posture both non-threatening and protective at the same time.

"We need to talk again," Debriah began.

"Meow," said Carousel.

"I need to go over those horrible events with you again. We must be overlooking something. Come on. Commune with me."

"I can't speak about it." Carousel swiped an eye with a paw.

"You must. There must be something more that you saw. I have always sensed a reluctance on your part to be entirely forthcoming about what you saw of the murderer."

"I'm pining for my person. I love her."

"I know and I understand. The faster we get to the bottom of the shootings, the sooner you can reunite with her."

"Well, there is one thing I have been reluctant to say."

Carousel sniffed the air as though catching a drift of Kitty Roasted Tidbit Cravings.

"What. Tell me. Please."

"My vision posed a problem that evening. I was seeing double."

"Seeing double?"

"Yes, um, well, that is the best way to put it."

"Carousel, you must describe to me exactly what you saw."

Debriah leaned over the cat, took her chin gently in her fingers and gazed into her eyes.

Carousel batted her lashes and told her story once more.

Chapter 27

Sunday afternoon Amy Raxel came to get Carousel.

"I'm sorry but I worry she will suffer environmental disruptive trauma if she stays with you any longer."

Amy shook a little, as though she feared Debriah would refuse to surrender Carousel to her.

She soon knew that while Samantha had been prepared to blackmail her to find Loyce, Debriah has no such scheme to keep Carousel.

"She is a very even tempered cat. But you are her person so I cannot go against your wishes."

"I cannot be without her for much longer. I need her. My pets are all the affection and caring I have in my life."

Now that she feared her exposure of her vampire activities, Amy had not liaisoned with any of her vampire support group members nor attended any meetings since Raize had visited her house.

She feared returning to Samantha since anonymously exposing Raize as a vampire in that impulsive phone call.

Dreadful isolation closed in.

Amy shivered.

Debriah nuzzled Carousel's neck as she fetched the animal for Amy.

"Did she tell you anything?"

If Debriah caught the sarcasm in Amy's voice, she did not let on.

She did notice a tremor subsided.

"Not much more than she first told me. I expect she knows more than she cares to admit, but she is afraid. She did reveal that she was having trouble with her vision. Seeing double. Has she had any trouble with her vision in the past?"

Carousel looked from one woman to the other with wide unblinking eyes.

"Seeing double?" Amy mused aloud to herself as she walked with the cat away from Debriah's front door. "No, she's never had any vision problems as far as I know."

The feline stretched in the front passenger seat of Amy's car. She flinched each instant the vehicle bounced and rattled. It was an old car.

"I wish I could talk to you," said Amy. "I mean, that you could talk back and I could understand you. I guess that's a mystery I'll never solve."

"Meow," said Carousel.

"If I could tell you what I saw and you could tell me what you know, then we could both get off the hook, right?" Amy did not watch for the cat's reaction but kept her eyes on the road as she drove.

Carousel yawned.

"Are you glad to be home?"

Carousel roused herself from a catnap as Amy carried her into a small manufactured home, white on the outside, but inside decorated with black carpet, black curtains, and black wallpaper.

Sniffing, she soon began swiping at the happy dog bounding forward to greet her.

"I'm glad to see you two have a happy reunion," said Amy.

The dog and cat sprang around the floor in mock battle.

Amy stared at a text on her licensed cellphone. Her permit level allowed for 20 calls per month, incoming or outgoing. An additional 20 messages, audible or text, were allowed.

Messages could be rejected prior to viewing so as not to count.

But Amy dared not.

The communication did not shock her but did surprise her with its stark directions.

"I fear no happy reunions for me," said Amy, and the bitterness in her words caused both her pets to stop and stare.

She flopped down on the couch like a broken mannequin.

Within seconds they were at her side, licking and nuzzling, comforting her as only they could.

Chapter 28

By Monday morning, Debriah was also suffering emotionally. She called Raize intending to tell him about Carousel's unusual revelation. She was tentatively planning to hold to her promise to Samantha to not mention Loyce's name in connection with the sexual role-playing enactment she had witnessed at The Men Unadorned Club.

Nevertheless, she thought she might tell him the identity of the man involved anyway if he insisted.

Plus, she had valuable information that Marlotta Holt was an owner of the club.

She wound up telling him nothing.

He had failed to return her calls.

Brooding about what she might have done wrong, Debriah had no idea the actions of another law enforcement officer were threatening her love affair.

"I can make it easy for you to erase your past," Electra had told Raize. "Marry me and all evidence that you ever had any vampire tendencies will be redacted from all government records."

"And suppose I don't marry you?"

Raize had to admit to himself that it was tempting to finally be free of records of this past that could be dredged up to haunt him. However, the edge in his voice alerted the FBI agent that marrying her was not amenable to the police captain at all.

She openly blackmailed him right then.

Wed her or be exposed as a vampire.

He remembered his encounter with Amy Raxel. She obviously sensed his secret. And of Samantha Speer and her open suspicions already shared with Debriah.

He knew he could not downplay all their accusations.

His superiors would be counting the number of accusers.

No claim of undercover activity would suffice.

He acquiesced to Electra's demands.

He would marry her.

"Excellent," she had replied. "I will get the license tomorrow and we can be married in the afternoon."

Raize anticipated Electra would be listening to his phone call to Debriah.

In addition, she would be stalking him.

He had to tell Debriah and tell her in a way that convinced Electra he meant it.

And he planned to. He had every intention of doing the right thing.

His past had come back to haunt him, threatening to cost him the first person he really loved. All hope for the future smashed due to his actions as a younger man.

He recalled the first occasion he had ever bitten a woman. The thrill and excitement of her flesh opening and blood seeping out.

He had not planned to taste it. But his tongue had swiped the wound.

The blood was so delicious.

Coincidentally, he had been dieting strenuously to make sure he did not exceed the legislated weight for his height. This was especially important since he wanted to serve his country.

The woman he had been with had not seemed to mind his unusual action.

However, he had not seen her again in fear that she would report him.

Instead he had taken to eating rare steaks, occasionally indulging in raw hamburger meat.

Then he began his clandestine life. Creating a separate identify for himself, he had entered a secret underground world where everyone wore black, slept all day, and roamed at night.

He considered himself a vampire and did all he could to prevent the outlawing of the movement during the great social upheavals of the last three decades.

A lonely existence followed, undertaken under an assumed name, due to the respectable position of his parents, both college professors in Kentucky.

A sad routine of protests and political harassment, broken only by his daytime activity working as a security guard to make ends meet, an endeavor that revealed his calling. Then he finally snared his dream job.

Cop by day, vampire by night.

That could not last.

He had sustained such a life for too many years.

Slowly he had detached himself from his nocturnal habits, buried all evidence of his vampiristic existence, living a celibate life for a long time.

Too long.

Debriah Brock represented his hope for the future.

She was so different.

So wonderful.

A hope for a family.

Both his parents were still alive and he communicated with them frequently on the phone but rarely had time to go visit them. He was an only child and his failure to give them grandchildren was a great disappointment to them.

Debriah was young and fertile.

Now Electra Simpson threatened to spoil his chance for a normal life.

He pulled out his weapon and cleaned it.

He pictured Electra's neck.

Short and solid.

He could break it with some difficulty.

He tested the mechanism of his gun as he finished the cleaning.

Shooting her would be much easier.

Chapter 29

Still not being able to contact Raize by late Monday afternoon, Debriah had gone to Raize's office again, planning to break her word to Samantha and tell him what they had witnessed concerning Loyce and The Male Unadorned Club.

In addition, she still planned to report that Marlotta Holt was at least one of the owners of the corporation.

He was not there.

No one would tell her his location or current activity.

Except he was betrothed to an FBI agent.

All his coworkers trumpeted his intention to wed Electra Simpson. They told her that with a celebratory air indicative of the expectation the news would stimulate a desire to congratulate him on Debriah's part.

Astonished and hurt, she staggered back home and flung herself down on her sofa.

Subsequently Monday evening, she received a simple sad call from Raize confirming his betrothal.

He tried to explain at length, starting by apologizing for the delay in informing her, but she hung up on him after a few short words.

Without pushing him for an explanation.

The stress resulting from Raize's intentions to marry Electra being so officially confirmed sent Debriah into a stunned state of mind.

She knew a time travel episode loomed, but she did nothing to fight it.

Let it come, she thought. *And may I never return to this cursed modern world.*

Debriah found herself in a huge building with towering racks of colorful objects, many in boxes with intricate artwork.

She stood still, stifling her anxiety.

She was hardly alone. Many others, most pushing wheeled silver colored metal receptacles, were perusing the displays, sometimes pulling an item off and tossing it into the cart.

These people were calm and acclimated. They did not seem to fear their circumstances nor were they trying to find a way to escape. As some disappeared at the end of the aisle, others took their spots.

A hum of casual conversation interspersed with soft music.

Debriah's panic subsided.

She studied the dress of the other people. Most wore pants and non-matching tops. Shoes ranged from sandals to boots.

People were more interested in the items displayed on metal shelves than in each other. Occasionally they politely acknowledged one another. Sometimes they spoke more than a few words. Attitudes were cordial.

Debriah nodded carefully to a woman who passed nearby.

Experience had taught her to be cautious.

She began to process the environment objectively.

From historical epics, remembered scenes brought triggered recognition of the setting.

She was in a retail store.

"Brick and mortar!" she murmured aloud causing a nearby shopper to glance at her with an odd eye.

How exciting!

She wondered what historical period.

"Pardon me." She spoke to the woman who just passed.

To her relief the woman replied in English.

"I don't work here," she said.

"I understand. But I wonder, do you have a phone?"

The woman cocked an eyebrow. "Certainly, but you cannot use it," she said.

"Oh," said Debriah, taken aback.

"I do carry a smartphone but there's no reception in here. These concrete buildings just block the signals. There's a payphone in the front lobby," said the woman.

"Thank you."

The woman pushed her cart away.

Debriah walked as calmly to the front of the store as she could, going about it the long way as she navigated the rear end first.

At the front she saw a stack of papers on a metal rack.

She took one. It was the store's advertisement and it would tell her the date.

Even more important- a newspaper stand. But those papers were not free. And she did not have any coins to put in the slot for payment.

Still, the headlines could confirm the date and help her cope until she could instigate her emergency medication, which would bring her back to the present.

Staring at the small container of newspapers she abruptly recalled the emergency medication. She had to keep her mind focused on it until she could trigger its absorption into her skin or she would forget it again.

She walked the length of the store once more, this trip finding the women's restroom.

Safely inside, she massaged the muscles in her left breast until the emergency patch activated and the medication released.

She relaxed.

Leaving the restroom, she enjoyed perusing the store, calculating she had up to 20 minutes to take in the past.

It was her first experience in the traditional brick and mortar store environment. She was thrilled.

She especially enjoyed the colorful toys. She stopped before a section of fashion dolls.

"That's the new set of the famous child actress triplets," commented a bystander with a basket full of dolls. "I'm a collector of celebrity fashion dolls, Barbie sized."

"Are you registered?" Debriah asked the question automatically.

The woman looked puzzled. "What?"

"Oh, uh, I mean, do you belong to a club? I also collect."

"No, I want to belong to one but I'm so busy. You?"

"No. Not here. Who are these?" Having trouble believing her own eyes, Debriah reached.

"Oh, I've been waiting for these forever!" The woman snatched the dolls off the shelf before Debriah could completely execute her own arm movement.

Happily, the store was well stocked.

Debriah picked up the set of three dolls representing very young girls, two identical and one decidedly different in facial features and body type.

"Three sisters?"

"The famous Fortune triplets." The woman was beyond enthusiastic. "They are on their own TV series. I'm ecstatic they were made into fashion dolls. I'm putting them right between Frank Sinatra and Carrie Fisher."

"I was not aware there were three Fortune sisters."

"My dear! Where have you been these past TV seasons? Two are identical and one is, well, not as attractive. Not that I watch the show much myself. It's the dolls that are important."

"You've acquired a lot of dolls?" Debriah asked to be polite.

"Over 300. All the British Royal family, all the Presidents and First Ladies. A few vintage Barbies but I mostly collect celebrities. If you are new to collecting, the Fortune triplets are a wonderful start. The dolls are sure to appreciate in value rapidly."

"I see." Debriah stared at the box in her hand.

"My dear, you look a little pale. Are you okay?"

"Oh, I, yes." Debriah moved away with alarm. Time had slipped by and the medicine was working. She did not wish to vanish before this friendly woman's eyes.

That would not be nice.

Hastily making her excuses, Debriah rounded a corner and scrunched down on a near empty paper towel display hoping she was not too noticeable…

Debriah often wondered what occurred as her visitations to the past drew to an end.

Do I disappear in front of people if I cannot get to an isolated area? Do they remember me? Do I leave evidence behind?

She did not know and could imagine no way to find out…

She awoke abruptly.

Unsure at first whether the adventure had been a dream or a

real episode, Debriah struggled to remember the details.

Sometimes they did not come to her for days, sometimes never.

She rose and turned on the light.

There on the bed Debriah beheld the evidence. Shoplifted from the past.

A real time travel episode.

Three dolls in a box stared at her.

Two identical, one different.

Chapter 30

Electra Simpson was not there to watch Debriah Brock exit the police department.

She was monitoring Raize's phone conversations, breaking the law listening to a fellow law enforcement official without his permission.

She listened to his abortive call to Debriah.

She heard enough to convince her that Raize intended to follow through on his promise to marry her.

Satisfied that objective was achieved, she endeavored to resolve an unrelated dilemma.

The FBI agent drove to The Men Unadorned club.

Electra entered the rear area of the club, reserved for employees.

Having rarely come in that way, disorientation swayed her. The place was such a maze.

Then she saw a familiar face.

"I have come to tell you the game is up. I know you have been helping people disappear and get new identities through this time travel scheme. I looked the other way. But murder is going too far. It has got to stop."

"You are going to stop us. That's a laugh."

"I know what has happened to Lars Holt and his flirt."

"You cannot possibly know anything. How could you?"

Electra hesitated. She wanted to say 'A witness has come forward.' But she did not want to say a cat witness.

"A cat told a tale-" She got no further. She heard hearing a shot and saw a flash.

She caught her breath. But relief flooded as no pain sensations materialized.

"Who else is in here?" she demanded. "Oh, it's you two. On the job training? Well this is good for you. Let's just see who's firing those shots."

She drew her gun and proceeded beyond her companions.

She gasped when the completely nude, completely shaven

man stepped in front of her. A rush of pleasure at seeing him again enveloped her.

She gazed in all the wrong places before seeing his gun.

Another flash blinded her. Taken off guard, she slipped. Her companions pushed her forwards and one tore her shirt collar from her neck…

The next morning Electra Simpson's body was found on the performance stage of The Men Unadorned Club.

The FBI called Captain Parks to the scene, as Electra's superior had known she was working with Raize.

He averted his eyes from the surroundings, not wanting to bring attention to the club, especially the office section.

He did not want Loyce Landers' infiltration of the activities behind the china cabinet nor the closet door entrance to the entertainers' private rooms revealed to Electra's cohorts.

The setting evidenced no real connection to the killing anyway.

The murderer had stripped Electra of life in some unknown location, then moved her.

Every detail of Electra Simpson's body was visible. She was totally nude, draped across a ringside table pulled up the singular step to the wide platform.

Electra's arms were outstretched, pulled by gravity towards the floor, as was her head, her distinctive features almost upside down with her hair falling from the crown of her head towards the floor. Her face was unmarred. Her eyes were closed.

Her neck showed signs of a jagged wound.

In addition, it contained the only blood on or in her body.

Her white torso spread across the center of the table, cleared by the impact of her blanched corpse. The only colors it held were her nipples and dark hair on her groin.

Her lower legs and feet were not clearly visible as they draped on the other side.

"Her smartphone is gone," said Raize and the normalcy in his speaking manner acted like a splash of cold water on everyone else.

But the officer bit his lip. The comment revealed too much. He glanced around to see who all had heard it and reacted.

Amy Raxel slumped in another chair ringside. A policeman pulled her up and dragged into the performance area, handcuffed.

"Tell this man to let go of me. She was already dead when I got here."

"Suspect resisted detention."

"Let her go, Officer. I'll deal with her."

Amy confronted a hostile Raize. She expected him to grill her about the dead woman.

Instead he asked, "where is the cat?"

"At home." Amy squirmed.

"Do I have your permission to get her? It is vital the feline be kept safe and you may be detained a long while by the FBI."

"I can handle the FBI. Just what is so important about my cat? I just got her back home."

Raize hesitated. Effects of the cat's tale had been minimized so far. No one knew that Carousel was witness to the murders except himself, Debriah, and he suspected, Samantha.

And one other. Electra Simpson had known…

"I'm not at liberty to say, just believe me when I say, she needs protection and should not be left alone at your house."

Amy handed Raize her keys.

"I want my pets to be safe more than anything in this world," said Amy.

As Electra's fellow FBI agents began interrogating Amy, Raize raced to her house.

A vivacious dog greeted him.

Carousel was nowhere to be found.

Chapter 31

"I was never going to marry her. It was just a clandestine operation. But I had to make you believe it."

Tension remained high between Raize and Debriah the next night…

Their relationship notwithstanding, Carousel's disappearance contributed an undercurrent providing much of the stress.

Underneath the anxiety, Debriah secretly thrilled that he was at her house, in her bed again.

She rejoiced that the competition with Electra Simpson was resolved.

Raize now belonged to her absolutely.

He stretched nude before her, also visibly thrilled.

"Now get undressed and stop acting angry." His physical happiness was threatening to explode.

"I am angry. I am hurt. Why couldn't you trust me?" Debriah kept her clothes on.

"I did trust you. I trusted you not to believe anything I said. Let that be a lesson to you. Anything I tell you in the office that ever indicates that our relationship is over or such, anything like that, you don't believe it!"

"I suppose I have to get used to having a secretive police captain for a lover."

He reached up and pulled her down to him by her blouse.

"Unbutton that at once."

And in an instant his face got lost in her breasts and she felt a little sting on each side. One following another.

"Stop biting," she fussed. "I need to get my pants off."

"Oh, you like it." He laughed as he helped her finish undressing, biting a little more with each action.

Then he grabbed her and the room spun as she felt him pulsate inside of her as he nibbled at her neck simultaneously.

"Oh, I love you, Raize!" she murmured as the pleasure overwhelmed her.

He fell into her arms and rested his chin on her shoulder,

relaxing.

"What are you thinking right now?" he asked dreamily.

"Well." Debriah rose up a little. "I'm so worried about Carousel."

Raize sighed deeply. "Why am I not surprised?"

"I'm afraid for her."

"She does have innate defense mechanisms."

"She's just a little kitty!"

"Shall we abandon our passionate love making and go look for her on foot? We can comb the woods calling 'kitty,kitty,kitty'. In the nude if you wish."

"Behave. She could be in danger. It's serious."

Raize got up and headed towards the shower. "It's serious, all right."

"I'm going to go over to Amy Raxel's place and see whether Carousel has not turned up there and is pining at an empty house."

"Don't bother."

"Why not?"

Raize searched for a fresh towel and turned on the water.

"She's agreed to let us know immediately if the cat makes an appearance. She will not welcome any company from me or you."

"What! Amy's free? They let her go?"

"In their infinite wisdom the FBI powers-that-be let her go."

"Why?"

"As Electra's murder was evaluated, Amy was released. Not a significantly inane decision on their part. It was determined Amy was unlikely to have killed the FBI agent, being too small and frail, Electra would have been a match for Amy under most any circumstance, but especially with a knife. Plus, Electra's blood went somewhere and Amy was blood free. No computer found on her either. Or in her car."

"So we don't know who killed your colleague."

"No."

"Any chance she took a Death Option?"

"No. She did not believe in life after death despite scientific proof."

"I see."

"It was also determined Electra was killed elsewhere, then taken to the stage and arranged in that provocative manner. And someone managed to break into her office and search it."

"Was anything taken?"

"How the hell could we know? She was not under any requirement to keep records. She was FBI. Anything could have been in that office and no one would know it. We do know the killer took her smartphone but has not used it. It will probably be sold on the black market. Likely to be smuggled out of the country before it's ever re-activated."

"So it could have been anybody? Any criminal she dealt with?"

"Yes. Except where her body was deposited ties it all in with my investigation. And keep in mind you must keep quiet concerning what I told you. I would be a prime suspect."

"Why, if it were part of an undercover operation?"

"The definition of undercover operation is that no one knows it is an operation. For all intents and purposes it was made to look as though I was being blackmailed by Electra Simpson."

"And you weren't?"

"Certainly not. What would there be to blackmail me about?"

"Your relationship with me."

"She knew nothing about that. Trust me. I was using her to get to DNA results the FBI had taken concerning the crime against Lars Holt."

"But she did know about Carousel witnessing the murders."

"Yes, but she did not believe it."

"Did not believe Carousel?"

"Did not believe cats can talk. She suspected you."

"Me?"

"Yes, because you alerted the police. But when no evidence of any shootings fitting the circumstances you described surfaced, she dropped it."

Just like they do psychics who report their visions. And I believed I was safe with animals, Debriah thought.

139

"And Marlotta Holt being an owner of the club. How does that fit in?"

"I don't know. You are sure about that?"

"Yes."

"It is valuable information, if so. I cannot fathom why Electra did not unearth it in her investigation. She should have known."

"Raize, who do you believe killed her?"

"I don't have any idea. The glaring question is how did the killer or killers get inside her office to ransack it?"

Debriah had not thought of that aspect of the murder.

"You don't know how?"

"There are only two ways. And DNA recognition would identify the killer or killers."

"Two ways? What other way could there be besides DNA recognition?"

"A key."

"Oh. But who would have a key?"

"That's just it. Few people. And I am one of them."

A key turned in Debriah's front door.

"That will be Samantha. She wants to see you."

Raize smiled. "Still worried about her missing boyfriend?"

Debriah hesitated. "She did not want me to tell you but we found out about him.

Raize tensed.

"You what?"

"I'll let her tell you. Get dressed. I asked her over here so we could confide in you unofficially. She is so embarrassed about it all."

Raize's blood pressure caused a pounding in his head that made him a little dizzy at the sight of Samantha.

"Shouldn't you be at the library?" The vampire consoler managed a skeptic smile.

"I might be headed there." Raize rubbed his temple.

"How do you find spending the night at the library?" Samantha persisted.

He kept his reply cordial. "It was actually nice. Dark and quiet. Peaceful. Solitary."

Debriah sensed tension. Unknown, but she tried to break it.

"I suspect Samantha is right. You are a vampire!" Debriah teased Raize.

Samantha jumped. "I did not say that," she said hastily.

"Yes she did." Debriah kissed him. "And I think he is the most desirable vampire ever."

"No need to flatter me. I love you anyway," he said to Debriah. And to Samantha- "and you better watch your language. Loose talk like that could cause trouble."

Samantha took a breath. She deflected her shock and disciplined her response.

"You don't need to frighten me, Captain. I am Debriah's friend. I don't care about your age difference."

"Debriah said you found your friend Loyce. May I ask under what circumstances?"

"I do not want to talk about it. Ever."

Debriah described to Raize what she and Samantha had seen under the guise of watching a time travel enactment.

"It was just role play enhanced by drugs. And he was deep into it. Enjoying himself." Samantha started to cry.

Raize rubbed his neck.

"What I am going to do is breaking all the rules, Ms. Speer. I'm going to tell you about Loyce."

Raize gave Samantha the shock of her life by revealing Loyce's true occupation.

"And you understand that if any of what you know, including my interactions with Debriah, become known, it could cost Loyce his life," he concluded.

"I am going to marry Loyce. I'll keep your secrets. All of them."

"Loyce is like a brother to me. I'm the one who took him from patrol officer and promoted him to undercover operations. I know he wants a traditional wife and family. But if I decide I cannot trust you-"

"I'll give you a little tip that may help you trust me."

"It would set my mind at ease to know you are with us."

"Then I will betray a client confidence. I had a young girl

141

come in the other day for counseling. She thought her disguise succeeded, but I know who she was. It was Bonita Holt. Someone in the army reported her. Not only is she the heiress to The Men Unadorned Club, she thinks she is a vampire."

"Samantha, just believing you may be a vampire is grounds for dismissal from the service, isn't it?" Debriah asked.

"Yes. Captain, I'm sure you know that fact. The military informed me that Bonita got involuntarily discharged and I might be required to testify if she appealed. Apparently she did not."

Raize looked reflective. He did not want to know how she became so informed.

"That's good information to know. So we now deal with the daughter of new proprietor of The Men Unadorned Club. A fired soldier vampire too young to patronize her own business. Well, if she plans to continue her exotic time travel operations in which people are actually purchasing false identities, I'll be back there soon."

"Don't you think Loyce is in danger, considering what Debriah and I viewed?"

Raize hesitated. He had made no communication with Loyce for a longer time than remained comfortable.

Until now he had not been concerned.

"Undercover operatives sometimes have to participate in unpleasant activities in order to conceal their true mission. But I'm sure he is perfectly safe."

Chapter 32

Loyce Landers regained consciousness, feeling cold and seeing only dark.

The room was no longer swaying.

He was still bound to the bed but the bonds were looser.

He did not feel any pain or significant discomfort.

Physically.

However, he fought mental collapse.

Horror kept him staring straight at the ceiling, especially not looking to his right.

He was no longer alone in the bed.

"Are you tied up?" he asked the figure beside him.

No response.

Loyce shut his eyes and turned his head slightly.

He opened his eyes slowly to try to filter in opaque rays from device indicator lights.

He could not see whether his companion was a man or woman but he could tell the victim, unlike himself, wore clothing.

Still no reply.

"Hey, wake up! Can you hear me?"

Loyce was cold and his companion was either wearing or blanketed by bulky material. He reached and, with movement limited by his bindings, pulled some of the cloth towards him to keep warm.

The figure rolled over slightly.

The dim light failed to assist his blurry eyes. He could not make out anything.

Therefore, he began to feel more.

He could move his hands a few inches at a time and work his way closer.

Still speaking soothingly to the person so as not to alarm him or her, he began to fear his fellow victim was unconscious, possibly drugged or badly hurt.

His hands encountered a satiny taffeta material for some distance before he touched skin.

He jumped.

Irrefutable cold evidence that the person was dead.

Loyce jerked at his bindings until they hurt.

Initially in silence.

Then he began to yell.

He alternated between 'help' and 'fire' hoping the latter would attract at least his captors.

Anybody.

He yelled for some duration before a spotlight blared on, blinding him in a different way.

"Shut up or I'll kill you."

"Ready to exercise your Death Option?"

He was unsure if both lines were spoken by the same person. They carried slightly differentiated accents.

Yet he could make out only one indistinguishable figure standing over him.

"Let me go." He voiced the words with despair because he knew that the speaker believed he could make an identification easily. "I cannot see you clearly. I don't know who you are. I couldn't identify you. Let me go."

The spotlight went off and a normal light flipped on.

Loyce's vision focused.

The killer appeared clear in the doorway.

Loyce had, by now, glanced at the dead person beside him, knowing he must be next.

"You, you can count on me. I don't pick any quarrels with French Dixie supporters."

"Think you know who I am, do you?"

He stared speechless at the murderer.

"We're still working on trying to find out who you are and why you finagled your way in here."

Incredible relief overcame Loyce.

They did not know who he actually was.

"I, I just want work."

"Maybe. We cannot excavate any trace of you. And unfortunately our operative for such chores is, um, no longer accessible. So we have to seek the truth the old fashioned ways.

Unfortunately we've been busy."

He looked from the corpse in the bed to the female alive several times.

The woman prepared another dose of opiate.

"You won't remember any of this, if you ever get out of here."

"No! Please!"

"Presupposing we don't kill you, you will be well compensated."

He was helpless as she forced another injection into his groin.

Confusion reigned almost immediately within his brain.

The woman massaged and kissed him.

"I would do more but it's the devil to get this dress off and on. I'm pressed for time and short on help."

Loyce could not resist turning to regard the figure beside him.

"She's not truly dead. But she's not exactly useful right now either."

The woman kissed him again and massaged him to the point of ecstasy.

"Maybe time travel is real. I am dead beside you but I stand above you. Maybe you have lost your mind."

The figure laughed, cut the light out, and slammed the door.

Loyce, again in darkness, battled for coherence and shrank as far away from the corpse as he possibly could.

He did not make another sound before passing out.

Chapter 33

Despite the unreliability of DNA evidence since scientists had invented ways of chemically altering it, the DNA results of all the persons of interest had told Raize that Amy Raxel was probably related to Marlotta Holt.

Somehow.

He still could not confirm Marlotta was an owner of the club. But he believed Debriah was correct.

Meaning Amy was more than an employee.

She was family.

Amy was the key to the operation at the club, Loyce Landers had suspected.

Raize attempted to reach Loyce. He was again unsuccessful.

Alarmed, Raize was now convinced Loyce had been correct about Amy.

Raize Parks pounded on the club manager's front door bright and early Wednesday morning.

When she opened her door slightly to address him, the police captain forced his way in.

"How dare you? What are you doing here without a warrant? I'll report you to your superiors. What do you want with me?" Amy demanded of Raize.

"I'll be asking the questions." Raize slammed the door behind him and grabbed Amy's arm as she reached to prevent him from advancing. "If I don't get satisfactory answers, I will take you back into custody and hold you for further questioning. I'm here on the most urgent business."

"Let go of me! I'm the one who needs protection. And I don't know where my cat is."

"I'm not concerned about the cat." Raize flinched inwardly as he spoke those words, glad Debriah could not hear him.

"Then what do you want?"

"Where is Loyce Landers?" Raize released her and stepped back. He wanted to view her in entirety to gauge her reaction to the question.

"Who is Loyce Landers?" Amy grabbed her elbows defensively.

"You know him as Loyce Smith."

"Oh." Amy relaxed. "That's what you are fishing for. Just another person to interrogate? What is he suspected of? He's just a dancer with no paper trail. Fooling around where he shouldn't be. And what do you have to offer if I tell you?"

Raize grabbed her by the arm and pushed her against the wall. He bared his teeth.

"If you know where he is you had better tell me at once."

"I'll turn you in," Amy said shakily. "I know you are a vampire."

"Turn all you want. It won't do you any good if you know where Loyce Landers is and you don't tell me."

"I- I only might know where he may be. Do you think something has happened to him?"

"He's missing, last seen inside The Men Unadorned Club."

"Missing?"

"Yes, and if you don't tell me where and how I can get to him, I'll lock you up whatever the consequences."

"Why is he so important?"

"Stop asking me questions! Where is he? I believe he is in mortal danger."

"That would be a first. If he has gone in for time travel work, he may be incommunicado. But no harm will come to him. Depending on which package he is participating in, he might suffer some fatigue."

"He would not have voluntarily participated in time travel."

"You'd be surprised. We do not overtly have much to offer men. But when they discover our covert activities, most take one package or other sooner or later."

"I tell you this man did not. But if I'm mistaken, if he did, where would he be?"

"I could lose my job."

"I know better than that. You're a relative."

"You think that shields me? It makes me more vulnerable. I'll

147

need to know you will keep me safe."

"Why do you need protection? What's going on at that club?"

"I don't dare say anything more. I cannot trust you."

"Forget me for the moment. If you need protection, I'm not the officer who will actually guard you. Now tell me. Where can I find Loyce?"

"You will send some ordinary policeman."

"Someone who will not even look at you twice."

"Suppose I tell you where I think Loyce is and he is not there, what will you do to me?"

Raize let her go. "Take your best shot. I will decide what to do with you later. But if you don't tell me promptly where you think he is, I'll make sure you never tell anyone anything again."

"I will need a bodyguard."

"You will have the best protection I can offer."

Amy believed him. Shakily she picked up a piece of paper and a pencil. "I'll draw you a map."

Raize scowled. "A map? A map to where?"

"A map of the true floor plan of The Men Unadorned Club."

Chapter 34

"An overdose of an aphrodisiac? Will I live?"

"Don't worry," an EMT told Loyce. "We have the Sexual Decompression Chamber waiting for you at the hospital. Herman, quick- emergency concealment device."

His partner snapped open a bag, popped a sheet out and shook it. In moments, the second EMT deftly covered Loyce strategically.

"The what?" Loyce's expression turned to alarm.

Raize interrupted.

"I must have a few more words with him."

"And you people are?"

The EMTs had found the nude Loyce surrounded by Raize, Debriah, and Samantha, the latter sitting on the bed beside Loyce holding his exterior in a comforting way.

The EMT's first action had been to pull Samantha away, then interacting with the victim, attempting to take control.

Loyce resisted the medical personnel. "I need more comfort!"

Raize flashed his badge at the two EMTs, causing them to retreat, muttering.

"How you must have suffered!" Samantha got back on the bed and cradled the now covered Loyce lovingly.

He snuggled against her.

Raize Parks had called Samantha as soon as Loyce had been located, a gesture she would never forget. She and Debriah had arrived at The Men Unadorned Club before medical help appeared.

Loyce had related that he had been tied to the bed for several days. Forced to participate in a role-playing sexual experience far more sinister than unwanted sex.

French Dixie characters brought to life.

Patrol officers materialized. Raize directed them to do a quick preliminary search of the building, while he and the women stayed with Loyce.

"And you were my audience, eating popcorn and drinking soft drinks?"

"We were told it was role-play, innocent theatre."

"Nothing is innocent when French Dixieism is involved," Loyce declared.

"No such thing as innocent theatre," Raize murmured.

"I will be haunted by those sex mad ghouls for the rest of my life," said Loyce.

Samantha focused on his distress. "Two women torturing you like that."

"It was awful."

Raize rolled his eyes, and had a sudden fit of coughing.

Debriah suppressed a smile.

"Which of them was the worst, darling?"

"Whichever one I woke up next to that was dead."

"Now you are sure that was not a hallucination?" Raize asked seriously.

Loyce had been alone in the bed when they had found him.

"Darling, do you want me to read a book to you?"

Loyce looked confused.

"Are you sure you did not recognize the two women?" persisted Raize.

"Were they identical?" asked Debriah, curious.

"I would not label them identical. They had, um, diverse styles." Loyce shifted as he recalled.

"If they were not identical it could not be the Fortune twins." Raize sighed with exasperation.

"Oh, they looked alike in the face."

EMTs had arrived at that moment, examining Loyce and pronouncing him a candidate for the sexual decompression chamber.

"Since Electra's dead, I will have no access to any computer files," Raize stated. "I can only submit an official request through a judge."

"Raize, it could be two of the Fortune sisters," said Debriah

"What do you mean?"

"We need to examine him and get him transported," said an EMT.

"Wait a minute," Loyce protested. "What kind of chamber?"

"I'll tell you later." Debriah spoke to Raize.

"Don't answer any questions," Raize instructed Loyce. "You are still technically undercover. And, Debriah, you cannot officially participate. So keep those meditations to yourself," said Raize.

"I guess that means you have to talk to the cat," said Loyce sarcastically.

"You think cats can talk?" asked one of the EMTs.

"Maybe he is going to need more than just one session in the chamber," said the other. "It could be he needs mental improvement consultation."

"I can handle that," said Raize to Loyce.

"Are you going to just let them take me?"

"Are you saying cat whisperers are fraudulent?" Debriah protested to the offending EMT.

"Technician, I'm the authority here. This is official police business and you are to ignore what you hear. No matter what this man says under the influence of any drugs, pay no attention."

"Raize!" Loyce gestured in alarm.

"And no one here is advocating any type of animal whisperers."

Raize gave a warning glance to Debriah that clearly directed *do not contradict me.*

She did not.

"You're wasting your efforts talking to the cat or me. I don't know any more. I cannot remember. Oh and I forgot about Amy Raxel. She knows the score. Talk to her," said Loyce.

The EMTs gave each other knowing looks.

"Can't remember? Memory problems?" asked one.

"We must prep him to be taken to the hospital for evaluation." The other addressed Raize again.

"She's the one who told us where you were." Raize responded to Loyce.

"Really? Voluntarily?" Loyce's eyes widened.

"Not exactly."

"Beware, she might be a vampire." The warning was a trigger.

"Vampire! We need to take him now." The EMTs were becoming aggravated.

151

One of them began fingering his gun holster unconsciously.

EMTs could use force if necessary but only when dealing with civilians, not law enforcement, which outranked them in the public control hierarchy.

A patrol officer entered, approaching Raize.

Raize abruptly gave in to the EMTs. He did not want any gunplay.

"Okay. Take him. Give him whatever treatment he needs."

"Raize!"

"Your duty is to cooperate with the medical authorities," Raize told Loyce.

"Thanks a lot! I hope you feel guilty at my funeral," said Loyce.

"I'm a therapeutic reader, I'm going with him," Samantha declared. "Loyce, I'll make sure you are not medically mistreated."

"Remember your duty," Raize said to Loyce.

"Captain, you need to see this." The patrol officer tapped Raize on the shoulder. "We've broken into another concealed room. And it is filled with illicit contraband."

As the ambulance departed, Raize and Debriah followed the policeman to a small closet disguised as a bathroom.

Inside were no plumbing facilities but hundreds of DVDs, assorted promotional items associated with popular entertainment, costumes copied from famous Hollywood designs.

Even two fashion dolls, identical one named Carlotta, and one called Marlotta.

Debriah beheld the dolls with delight.

"Now, Debriah. What were you talking about?"

Debriah informed Raize about all she knew about the famous Fortune triplets.

"Three sisters? You are sure?"

"Wait here for me until I can get something, okay?"

Debriah went to her car and returned with the boxed set of dolls.

"I've been carrying these with me, waiting for just the right setting to show them to you," she said. "Look, this proves it. There were three sisters, later only two sisters."

"This proves there were three dolls, later only two dolls," said Raize. "This may not have been based on reality."

"Back in that day it would have been. Note- one is shorter and heavier. They called it political correctness then. True to life."

"So?"

"These can solve the crime."

"First cats, then dolls are doing my job these days."

"I mean studying them."

"Where did you get these dolls?"

"They belong to a private collector. They are legal." Debriah was acutely uncertain about this but her pause was brief. "These illustrate Carlotta Fortune and Marlotta Holt had a third sister. That sister is bound to be the third owner of The Men Unadorned Club and its time travel subsidiary."

"Maybe the third sister, allowing she exists, is the third owner." Raize rubbed his hands together.

Debriah scanned one of the tapes again.

"The women Loyce saw could be the fraternal sister and one of the others," Debriah concluded.

As they huddled in the fake bathroom, conversation ceased. Raize and Debriah began sorting through a mountain of toys and entertainment as FBI forensics swarmed the greater crime scene to determine if there had really been a dead body in bed with Loyce.

Chapter 35

Thus began a race against time.

Raize had no interest in most of the memorabilia, promptly commandeered by the FBI, with plans to trace copyright holders who could claim it or destroy it.

Confiscation agents arrived at the club and left with several large boxes in record time.

Debriah watch sadly as the Barbie-type dolls of the identical Fortune sisters as adults slipped out of her fingers.

They would be so great in my fashion doll collections… At least I got to see them, to hold them…

Left behind were human sized French Dixie garments, which were to be shipped to a forensic seamstress analyst to investigate connections to manufacturers and distributors in hopes of securing prosecutions.

Raize claimed the authority to examine those items prior to relinquishing custody.

The FBI did not object.

However, all DVDs of all kinds had to be destroyed along with all videos promptly to prevent copyright infringement.

Raize procured an emergency court order to view all DVDs connected to the Fortune triplets before they had to be burned and catalog all the French Dixie costumes prior to sending them to the seamstress.

Cataloged were all the works of Carlotta Fortune, Marlotta Fortune, and Darlotta Fortune's careers. The last two being few in number before Marlotta married Lars Holt and Darlotta disappeared.

This included episodes of the TV series they had starred in as adolescents and the classic movie which made Carlotta a timeless icon, *Twilight of the French South.*

The judge gave him six hours to view hundreds of hours of tape. He received permission to allow someone else to operate the player.

He took the chance of giving Debriah that task rather than a police officer. Fortunately, no one questioned his decision.

The FBI was pleased that he offered his office for the destruction, saving them from the chore. Raize's workspace had a fireplace, which was for more than just heat in the winter, installed when shredders were outlawed,

Raize presented Debriah as the required random member of the public brought in to act as a witness in case any duplicates turned up later, throwing the destruction of the tapes into doubt.

The FBI agents helped transport the evidence to Raize's office, rigged a timer for six hours, and left.

Raize and Debriah spent that precious time fast-forwarding the TV videos in a marathon session but came away from them knowing little more about the sisters. Two child stars were precious duplicates, cute and lovely. The third actress bore them little resemblance. She appeared pudgy, plain, and her personality aggravated.

"Unfortunately, we don't have another six hours to run through the movie. But you have seen it, right?"

As they disconnected the player and packed the DVDs in the fireplace, Debriah summarized the movie in detail.

"I think we made the correct decision to watch the TV shows."

The deadline was up.

FBI destruction agents arrived to supervise the burning of the contraband.

As soon as the fire passed the point of no salvation, the FBI personnel prepared to leave. Raize asked Debriah to stay and clean up while he briefed them on what he had watched as he walked them to their transport.

When he returned, he and Debriah would search through the costumes and memorabilia, labeling each item, and taking notes as they packed it all for shipment.

Debriah began arranging items and tags as she waited for Raize to return.

She could not resist trying on one of the French Dixie formals. Sewn of illicit moiré satin in yellow, the taboo dress looked to be just her size. The formal gown was simple in style with no lace or other adornment yet its sensual cut with contrasting pouffy off-the-shoulder sleeves made it enchanting.

She wondered. Perhaps she could get away with swiping it. The costume was so comfortable. Moreover, it was practical for its day. Obviously a formal, it still had deep pockets. The dress gave her such an uplift, she wondered how she looked.

She pulled a small mirror out of her purse but could not see much with it.

She slipped down the hall to the ladies' room where there was a full-length mirror on the wall of the foyer entrance, which also boasted a small sofa and large makeup mirror with seats in front.

Debriah was extremely pleased with the way the gown made her look younger.

They knew how to dress for the best effect back then. No wonder the fashion movement grew into such a monumental cause, she reflected as she swished the skirt before the mirror.

I'm supposed to feel emotionally altered by this type of clothing, she recalled.

Incredulous at first, she began to feel light headed.

The perfumed air in the restroom foyer struck at the same moment that fumes from the fire clogged her airways. Chemicals often caused allergic reactions and sometimes her system did not alert her to the danger until after the exposure ended.

Dizzy, she clutched her chest and checked to see if she had a capsule in her purse.

She knew something in the chemicals was triggering a time travel episode but she was powerless to stop it. She managed to fish out one of the medicated patch that would bring her back and secret it in her bosom but she did not get a chance activate it.

Her only hope was that it could somehow be warmed by her body and be slowly absorbed by her skin as the episode progressed.

If this has to be, let me end up somewhere that gives me some insight to these murders, she prayed.

Chapter 36

Her prayers were answered.

Debriah found herself on a movie sound stage, dressed in a yellow French Dixie gown, her gold cross necklace exposed by its off-the-shoulders, deep cut bodice. Similarly styled people swished by her, all in a hurry, while a short bearded man barked instructions.

"All extras take their seats at the banquet table and just eat in a genteel manner while the actors and actresses play the scene. This includes you, lady."

"This way. You must be new." A tall friendly man took her by the arm. He was attired impeccably in the dominant style, accented with a top hat.

"I am new. This is my first extra job."

"Just follow along with me. Watch the others and act as natural as possible while remembering the theme of the movie."

"Um, sir. I forget. What is the name of this movie?" Debriah was sure she stood on the set of *Twilight of the French South*. However, she liked to get verbal confirmation of locations in her time travel episodes. It was easy to be fooled.

"*Vanished with the Hurricane*."

"What?"

"Just tentative, sure to be changed upon distribution. Just like this scene. It's a retake after the movie is practically in the can. They will cut out the original and insert this one providing it turns out better."

"Oh."

"Now just pay attention to his directions. Don't speak, just behave like everyone else and you'll do fine."

The friendly top-hatted man moved to his place with the other men, maintaining eye contact with Debriah as he pointed to the director.

Debriah nodded at her new friend, then turned to pay attention to the short bearded boss.

The director perched on a ladder. Sweeping his free arm across a long lavishly endowed banquet table with high backed chairs and an enormous chandelier hanging precariously over the center, he spoke through a handheld microphone.

"Now this is the action. As you gentle folk are eating a fine meal in elegance, soldiers will enter from stage left, drag Carlotta Fortune -uh, her character, that is- from the table, take her over to the next set, put her on the guillotine blade.

"Now you are all upset by this, but also very curious. You know the soldiers mean no harm to you so you do not panic but rather react as a crowd with intense interest and start to follow them out the door into the courtyard. Some of you need to react with horror to the guillotine. Others just react with amazement. Some protest, but very little, as they drag her to the scaffold and execute her."

"I hear she is going to exercise her Death Option," a female extra posing as a French Dixie aristocrat gossiped to Debriah.

She was seated to Debriah's right.

"I heard that was the plan," Debriah replied.

"I hope so," said a woman on the other side of Debriah. "I so want to watch somebody die for real."

"Well-"

"Better eat something, if you want some of this exquisite gourmet food before we are directed to get up and follow the soldiers," advised the first woman.

The others were all eating away.

Debriah took a bite

She tasted divine edibles. Beef melted on the tongue, vegetables flavored to perfection. Bread like heaven with pure butter.

The food tasted so good that Debriah was not paying any attention to the actors' dialogue until there a loud screech sounded and the violent action commenced.

Just as dessert was being served.

Ice cream!

Debriah had not had any authentic ice cream since it had become illegal during her childhood.

She hated to leave such incredible pleasure. She was one of the last to tear herself from the table, spoon in mouth.

My ice cream, she mourned miserably as the crowd of extras swept into the second set.

Debriah abruptly remembered what was going on and used the confusion to slip around to the other side of the locale.

There she beheld an interesting sight. Identical to the woman being hauled up the steps to the scaffold stood another woman in the same costume, with fake blood all over her neck.

The substitute corpse was impatiently tapping her foot in boredom as the hysterical actress was dragged onto the scaffold.

A stunning power failure caused instant confusion.

Frighteningly in the dark a few flashlights and cellphones gave out a little spooky lights. Chaos reigned as the director screamed orders to immediately activate emergency power.

His directive was fulfilled in seconds.

The lights blared back on. Debriah looked around. The bloodied duplicate was no longer in her sight but presumably at the foot of the guillotine.

Her head did appear to be severed from her body. However, sheets cloaked her so quickly as the film began rolling again Debriah was convinced the image was an illusion.

The unbloodied actress who had simultaneously stood at the guillotine while her perfect double waited soaked in red makeup was nowhere to be seen.

A popping noise caused Debriah to jump. She ducked behind a stage flat and inside a cubicle, which served to hide a plethora of props.

An automatic light in the enclosure revealed a number of DVD tapes, labeled with colorful pen marks.

"Preliminary copy," read one.

"Our day," read another.

The flat collapsed and the cubicle door flew open.

"What are you doing in here? Who are you?"

"Assistant stage hand. Just, um, just getting these DVDs." She hastily rushed beyond the uniformed security guard, pushing the DVDs in her pocket.

"Miss Fortune," called the guard. "Come over here."

As Debriah gazed in that direction of the actress, a figure

sprang up behind her.

"What are you doing back here? Who are you?" demanded an angry voice.

"Probably a journalist infiltrating the set. Grab her, Darlotta!" called the actress.

Debriah had the presence of mind to activate her medication just before the person with the menacing tone struck her on the head.

Wonder what they will think if I disappear right in front of their very eyes? Actually it would serve them right, was her last thought as she passed out.

Chapter 37

Debriah came to in the restroom. She quickly made her way back to Raize's office

The fire smoldered still.

The top of her head hurt.

Quickly she changed into her normal clothes, but not before she retrieved two thin disks from the pocket of the dress.

"They are gone, finally," said Raize, reappearing at that instant. "I thought they'd never leave. They demanded every blasted detail and were perturbed that the tapes were fast-forwarded. What choice did I have with only 6 hours to screen them?"

"Raize, would you be angry to know a couple of tapes got left behind."

"Now that could not be possible. I had to check every one off the list as it was put in the fire, remember. Nothing was left."

Debriah smiled.

She produced a commercial DVD of *Twilight of the French South*.

"How on earth did you get that by them? They all burned. I saw it!"

"My secret. Let's watch them."

"There's nobody to stop us right now."

Raize reconnected the player to his screen, flipping a switch so the viewing would be private.

They soon realized the decision to forgo screening the film to scan the TV shows had been a serious error.

The DVD was a rough cut of the film, sans title or credits but with many key scenes including a take of Carlotta Fortune's death scene.

As Carlotta was being beheaded in the film, a scene advertised as the true-life demise of the actress exercising her Death Option for realism, a tiny glitch could be discerned in the execution.

There was a brief second where the scene jumped.

"It was faked. No wonder they needed a retake," Debriah declared.

"How shocking." Raize kept a straight face.

Debriah glared at him. "Millions bought expensive tickets for *Twilight of the French South* just because of that scene. And it was a fake!"

"Do you really believe these actors and actresses, or politicians, or any famous and wealthy people actually exercise their Death Options and die on purpose. No, the only people who do that are ordinary people and public servants who have been conned into the idea that somehow by dying they are furthering some cause they believe in or their family will be better off for the experience."

"It is disheartening. Like finding out that meteorologists cannot really control the weather," said Debriah.

"Yes. Exactly. During my relationship with Electra Simpson, she did clue me in that many Death Option choices are faked, and sometimes the fatalities are not faked but they weren't voluntary either. Murder is involved."

"It is hard to believe. Unreal!"

"Unreal? This from the woman who talks to cats."

Debriah ignored the dig. "Do you think that Carlotta lived here all the time, playing double to her sister, Marlotta?"

"I would say so. She lived her life sharing an identity with her more practical and intelligent twin."

"A great talent whose only outlet is a repeated performance in secret as her character from her one famous movie. How sad."

"But here it is all on old DVD tapes. We just have to line them up and follow the story. It is all here."

"Now if Loyce is right, one of them is dead."

"Yes, but which one?" Raize asked.

"Let's watch the other tape."

The couple soon comprehended the second DVD documented a wedding.

Marlotta and Lars Holt's wedding.

And there, a long time beyond her supposed demise, was Carlotta, serving as bridesmaid for her sister."

"And look who else is there!" Raize exclaimed.

"That must be the third sister."

"Look, we are seeing the third sister only as an adolescent. She looks so familiar. The other bridesmaid at the wedding resembles an overweight Amy Raxel," Raize observed.

"But Amy Raxel is too young to be the third sister."

"She must have had plastic surgery and lost a lot of weight. She might have legally reduced her age."

"Remember the third sister was not from the same embryo."

"If so, then she made a fool out of me," said Raize, gruffly.

"I wish I could have kept those dolls!" Debriah lamented.

"They were unrelated to French Dixie? Just plain dolls of the actresses, manufactured earlier than the movie, you think?"

"Yes, but-"

"Let's look at the triplet set. Does that odd one look like Amy?"

The couple scrutinized the unattractive fashion doll silently for a moment.

"I guess so." Debriah's tone indicated uncertainty.

"I do see some faint resemblance. But why give the club's best secrets away? Why direct us to Loyce?" Raize wondered.

"Maybe she does not want anyone harmed. Carousel seems to regard her highly."

"The cat's judge of character notwithstanding, something Amy knows or saw frightened her. That is the only logical explanation, whether she's the third sister or not. She manipulated me into giving her protection. She's afraid," Raize concluded.

"Of what?"

"That I don't know."

"Why would she do that? Why not just take an assumed name and blend into society?"

"She may have had something else to hide. Perhaps she was into her role too much and was a supporter of the Dixie French terrorists. That would explain the disappearances at The Men Unadorned Club. An underground travel route for terrorists about to be exposed allowing them to get out of the country or assume new identities."

"So are you still on that case?"

"No, that is all under the auspices of the FBI and Electra's designated successor. But Lars Holt and Magdalene Rene Watters are my concern," Raize stated.

"You think Marlotta or Carlotta killed them all?" asked Debriah.

"My theory is this. It would be easy to pass as her sister Marlotta. They would just have to make sure no one saw them together or in conflicting situations. Carlotta could then not legally exist and hide any terrorist activities using Marlotta's identity. As the wife of a deliverer, Marlotta's social position was above reproach, even if it did come out that she was a business owner. That might bring her down a little but not much."

"So what went wrong?" Debriah asked.

"The real question is, why kill Lars?"

Debriah closed her eyes for a second.

"I might have a theory." She spoke with great hesitation.

"Go for it. I'm open to anything. Even clairvoyance."

"Let's say you are right about Carlotta Fortune being alive and Marlotta aiding and abetting her. Let's say both of them were in on the killings."

"Interesting. Go on," Raize prompted, encouragingly.

"When her existence is threatened by her brother-in-law's knowledge of the situation, Carlotta kills him. She happens to pick a time when he has his mistress in the house with him."

"She's unaware of this?"

"Yes. You say the girl was killed coming downstairs?"

"So say forensics." Raize folded his arms noncommittally.

"Let's say Carlotta kills Lars Holt, unaware Magdalene is there. She calls her sister, informing her that her husband is dead."

"Okay, that could be the phone call Loyce overheard. So in your theory, is Marlotta happy about her husband being killed by her sister?"

"Maybe. Probably not. But when Marlotta rushes to the scene, she discovers her husband's lover and becomes Carlotta's accomplice. Together they dispose of the bodies. Later, Carlotta is killed by Marlotta." Debriah opened her eyes.

"Marlotta killed Carlotta? Why?" Raize sounded perplexed.

"She got the life insurance upon Carlotta exercising her Death Option. Her sole beneficiary was her sister, Marlotta."

Raize was silent.

Debriah waited with difficulty.

"Interesting," said Raize. "Was all that a psychic insight?"

Debriah shifted uncomfortably. "No more than your theory."

"Mine is somewhat based on years of experience."

"And an instinct for detection?"

Raize scratched his chin. "The two theories do fit together. How does the third sister fit in, do you think? Any psychic theories about her?"

Debriah had to stop herself from replying that no inferences concerning the third sister had materialized in her brain.

"No. Who was the third sister?" she asked.

"I still don't know. But I'm sure I now know who does."

Chapter 38

"Carlotta Fortune still alive? Ridiculous."

Amy Raxel was home Thursday morning.

She was less hostile to Raize Parks than he expected when he relieved the patrol officer assigned to guard her.

This time she invited him in and even gave him a weak smile at his first accusation.

"I am the not the third sister. I am a cousin. The poor cousin of the Fortune triplets. I grew up in their shadows as a child. As an adult, they condescended to letting me know about their business. But I only managed the club. I had no financial interest in it. How did you know I was related to them?"

Raize had a ready story. He was not about to tell her about the videos.

"Your cat was indiscreet."

"That cat! I suppose you think I actually believe a cat told that to a cat whisperer? But I know you cannot make it stand up in court, however illegally you obtained your information."

"I can assure you my information was obtained through legal channels, Ms. Raxel."

"Oh, I can easily prove I was not their sister. Yes, I resembled the dissimilar one a little. I suppose my DNA is comparable."

"Similar enough that if the old DNA has been only slightly chemically tampered with, you could be the sister."

"I admit I am a relative. I'm a first cousin."

"And just happen to be involved in all their activities."

"Oh no. They kept me in the dark, always at arm's length. Fraid I would want more money."

"Did you blackmail them?"

"No, they would have not let me. Fact is, I had nothing to do with them after the television episodes ended. They worked steadily between the TV show and the famous movie. Carlotta became a moderate star. Marlotta, of course, got work as her stand-in at first. The other sister was too fat and short. Marlotta could not act her way out of a closet. But Carlotta was talented. For a few months, the other two tried to ride her success and the idea of them being triplets to fame."

"It didn't work?"

"It didn't work for Darlotta and Marlotta no more that it worked for me. I had neither the talent nor the looks. There was no job for me when I grew up. But later after Carlotta faked her execution and they got a fortune in life insurance, they took pity on me and hired me to manage the club they bought."

"And the third owner. Who is Darlotta? Where is she? If it is not you then you had better tell me the real identity, I'm warning you, Ms. Raxel."

"Didn't my cat tell you who?" Amy smirked.

"No, um. No." Raize had to stop himself from adding, *she didn't know…*

"It was Electra Simpson."

"That's impossible."

"Think about it. Check out her DNA."

"As an FBI agent, her DNA is classified even after death."

"I see. Well, she was the third fraternal triplet. The odd girl out. The Fortune triplets had a successful TV show but everyone could see there was no future for the one who was overweight and could not sing or act. So Darlotta was significantly disenfranchised, so to speak. She decided to go into government service."

"So from the period the TV series ended and until *Twilight of the French South* was made, the triplets were in decline?"

"Yes. Marlotta married well. She was able to slip away and lead a quiet life as a respected deliverer's wife. And surreptitiously go into business with Carlotta since Carlotta faked her death."

"Then they did not let Darlotta in on the business at first."

"By that time, Darlotta had ceased to exist. She had gone almost straight from the TV series to the bureau. As TV series teleplays were being destroyed by that time, she did not even need to fake a Death Option. She was just erased and forgotten. Born again as FBI agent Electra Simpson. I think they did a little plastic surgery to mask the resemblance to her sisters. Carlotta became so famous."

"Later you say Electra Simpson got in on the business? How?"

"Simple. She had access to identities of corporate entrepreneurs. Somewhere in the course of her work she discovered who owned the club. She blackmailed her sisters and they had to let her in. In exchange, she was able to secure certain favors and coax certain officials to look the other way when they began their more unseemly adventures."

Raize became silent. He was well acquainted with the late FBI agent's blackmailing tendencies.

"So, Mr. Brilliant Cop, satisfied?"

"And those adventures? You had better tell me if you don't want to wind up in jail."

"They called it exotic time travel. For most, it was just a sexual experience in costume. But for others it was a way to a new identity. I'm not sure how they did it. That's all I know."

"I don't believe that's all you know."

"Will you leave now? You cannot prove I murdered anybody. You cannot prove any fraud concerning the time travel. You are harassing me for no justifiable reason. I think you want your girlfriend to take my cat. Well, she's not going to. I love Carousel. I am well within my rights not to let her in the house if I don't want to. The Supreme Court says so."

Raize flinched. He suspected Amy's remark about Debriah constituted a shot in the dark. But he could not take that chance.

She was a shadow of her famous cousins in that she had no qualms about blackmail, fraud, or deception. But was she strong minded enough to kill?

He was not sure.

"I am going to go to a judge to try to get Electra's DNA information. Upon confirmation your story is true, you will be compensated for your information. I will send a patrol officer back to guard you."

Amy walked to her front door and opened it wide.

"Don't bother. I refuse police guards as of right now."

"But you asked for it."

"I was mistaken. I am in no danger. I don't want any cops to come back here. I am within my rights to refuse."

"Yes. That is true."

"So it is time for you to leave."

"Not quite yet. If you know for certain that one of the identical sisters killed Electra, you must tell us. It is your only chance."

"Another warning? You cannot threaten me. I don't know, I tell you. I found Electra dead on the performance platform. How or where she died, I've no idea. Now may I have my cat returned home for the last time? She cannot tell you anything either. I will go and get her right now as soon as you say I can."

"No you cannot do that. We don't know where the cat is."

Raize had the uncomfortable duty to comfort Amy for she began to cry.

Chapter 39

"When will I see you again?"

Debriah had not seen Raize since Wednesday.

Using a precious phone call allowance, she was questioning him Friday.

He was telling her it would be Saturday afternoon before they could meet again.

"The prudent action is to spend tonight in my library bed. And I'm going straight to work tomorrow. Some Saturday overtime just for appearance's sake."

The police captain was able to proceed straight to work Saturday morning without leaving the library premises.

Raize Parks himself found the bodies of Lars Holt and Magdalene Rene Watters unexpectedly…

Behind the curtain, inside a library bed in the basement.

By lunch the identifications were processed, forensics had taken over. Raize had the unpleasant duty to inform the next of kin.

Telling Magdalene Rene's grandparents was simple.

Since it was Sunday, he broke the news over the phone as gently as possible to the elderly couple.

Their undeniable devastation easily conveyed over the line.

Yet they refused emergency counseling, insisting they could handle their grief. Raize gave them the number for grief support anyway and instructed them how to claim the body.

Attempts to reach Marlotta Holt or her daughter, Bonita, were unsuccessful.

He left messages. Then he took the rest of the day off.

Drained emotionally, he slipped back to Debriah's house as planned.

As he arrived, Carousel materialized at Debriah's front door.

Debriah was ecstatic.

Exclaiming with happiness, she ushered cat and man inside, then she grabbed Carousel and passionately embraced her.

"Your joy results from my return, correct?" Raize kissed Debriah's forehead as kitty purred in her arms.

"She's been missing! She could have been dead!"

Debriah curled up with Carousel on the sofa. Raize plopped down beside them.

"What's happened?" Debriah demanded.

He recounted the morning events as briefly and with as little detail as possible.

"So do we think these are the people Carousel saw murdered? I hope she doesn't have to face the trauma making an identification."

"They fit the description one hundred percent. But since we know who they are, her observations are only useful unofficially. I doubt she will need to view the bodies."

Debriah reflected on that day Carousel had first narrated her story and how deeply moving it had been.

With so much happening so fast, her sadness about the deaths of the lovers had blurred.

Empathy returned sharply.

"Whoever killed them deserves an involuntary Death Option," she declared.

"I agree."

"So the killer moved their bodies after Carousel left the house. And put them in a reading bed at the library?" Debriah cuddled with the cat as she spoke.

"A double bed. Somehow their bodies were smuggled into the more expensive section. Logically in clothing bags found stashed under the mattress. The bed was rented with cash for an extended stay paid in advance."

"And how did no one come across them in all this time?" Debriah asked.

"They were in the Ancient Egyptian Section. A deluxe mummy experience is included with that package," said Raize. "The beds have lids that automatically fasten, then can be unlatched only from the inside for maximum privacy."

"Who do you think killed them?"

Raize took the feline from Debriah's arms, held the animal up by the shoulders and made eye contact.

"Can you account for your whereabouts, feline?"

171

"Meow."

This brought a rebuke from Debriah. "Put her down! She's stressed."

"She's always stressed, according to you."

"It will be years before she gets closure concerning the brutality she witnessed."

Raize put Carousel beside him and she promptly began to bathe.

"The library allows participants in that section to bring a cat for an extra fee. And this kitty has no alibi. Officially, her whereabouts are unaccounted for."

"Very funny," said Debriah. "I presume all the people have been accounted for?"

"We cannot locate anybody at present except the Watters couple. Not even Marlotta Holt to identify her husband's body."

"You know, we are ignoring a pertinent question. Who was the body Loyce claimed was in bed with him?"

"We are not focusing on Loyce's recollections since that body has never shown up. He was drugged."

"But if he was right and it was one of the identical Fortune sisters, does that make the other the killer?"

"Deducing either Marlotta Holt or Carlotta Fortune is still missing, not both."

"And, if Carlotta or Marlotta, not Amy, are the killers, or just one of them, who is next?"

"Amy Raxel."

"Why her?"

"She's refused protection. She knows something. She has an alibi for the deaths of Lars Holt and Magdalene Watters. She led us to Loyce, then abruptly stopped cooperating."

"I can alibi Carousel," said Debriah. "Watch what you say about her. Carousel could never kill anything. Think about the harm to her reputation."

"We are talking about a cat. Consulted with any bird whisperers lately? Of course she could kill."

The two people looked down at the feline, who was demurely

cleaning her claws.

"It's just the size of the prey that makes a difference," said Raize.

"You're theorizing a cat cannot commit homicide?" Debriah asked.

"Only in her fantasies. She is a small cat. Not much bigger than most kittens."

Raize indicated abnormally small kittens with dramatic hand gestures.

Carousel paused in her hygienic activity to glare at Raize.

"Does she understand what I say?" he asked.

"Probably not. She can only understand a few people with my condition, er, talents, and only when we are mentally in tangent." Debriah scratched Carousel's chin.

The feline purred.

"You know, I'm not sure I can cope with a cat and a cat whisperer. Maybe we should take Carousel back to Amy Raxel when this is all over."

"I cannot let Amy Raxel take Carousel back. Ever. She may be a killer. Don't you have a duty to safeguard her? Carousel is a material witness."

"Animals cannot testify in court. Not even cats. I'm supposed to be protecting Amy Raxel. She asked for protection, accepted it for a while, then rejected it after my last visit to her. That is worrying me."

"So there's no one at her place now to protect Carousel. The potential for harm to Carousel is too great. Sorry but I know my duty. I can testify as to what Carousel tells me."

"Whisperer testimony rarely stands up in court."

"What about time travel experiences?"

"Why do you ask that?"

"Just curious."

"Totally impermissible in court. No judge would admit any testimony that emerged from a time travel trip and I hope they never will. I believe it's all a scam done with drugs and role-play. Just what's going on at The Men Unadorned Club?"

Debriah bit her lip.

Here was an excellent opportunity to tell him about her Time Travel Syndrome.

She could not do it.

"Why don't you arrest them then?"

"It is a very gray area in the law. Drugs are legal. Role-play is legal. Theatre is legal."

"What about photographing people? I would expect video devices would automatically be prohibited."

"Not if they are recording deactivated. Video devices can be used for projecting copyrighted scenery. People under the influence can easily be tricked."

"I would assume that would be fraud."

"There's only a fraud if the participant is somehow duped or harmed. Most victims are unwilling to admit they were stupid enough to believe they actually traveled back in time."

Debriah was silent.

"Speaking of traveling I am going to have to go soon. I'm staying here too many hours. Sooner or later someone is going to notice me."

"Oh?" Debriah was immediately let down. "I miss you all the hours you are not here."

Debriah knew they were becoming bolder.

It was risky.

"Are you going back to the library to stay?"

"All beds have been emptied and closed for forensic analysis in anticipation other crimes have been missed. The library is only open for checking out books right now."

"Strange. Like the old days. I hope that doesn't last, people with insomnia will be forced back to drugs."

As he left, she hugged Carousel.

"Carousel, what do you think of Raize? You like him?"

Debriah whispered the questions to the feline.

Carousel did not answer.

I already know too much about both of you, the feline was thinking. Her eyes slitted. She napped.

Chapter 40

Amy Raxel had decided she was finished with fear.

I am indestructible, she reminded herself. *I need no protection. I am infallible.*

I going to be more important than just the manager of The Men Unadorned Club.

After Raize Parks departed she contemplated and reassessed her position.

Saturday morning her plans crystallized.

She sought out the person who could make this happen.

She believed she had accumulated enough blackmail material to force terms on her.

The club was still closed but there was activity on the premises.

"I demand part of the profits," she told the person in front of her.

"I always thought it was a mistake to make you manager here."

"It was your mistake, or maybe it was Marlotta's and you are Carlotta. I don't care. But I know now there are two of you. What I saw the night Electra died makes sense. You are both still alive."

"You idiot! You dream you can threaten us!"

"Mother, what is the trouble?"

Bonita entered the club through the rear, veiled as always to disguise her young age.

She knocked at Amy's office door but did not wait for an acknowledgment of her rapping before entering.

"Just a minor conflict among family."

Bonita slipped an arm around Amy's waist.

Marlotta pursed her lips. "Tell Cousin Amy I am your mother."

Bonita laughed. "Amy, it's easy to tell them apart. Aunt Carlotta is crazy."

"So you know Carlotta is still alive?"

"Not until I got home from camp and found out my father was missing."

"So you think Carlotta is behind your father's disappearance?"

"Shut up, Bonita."

"We don't know what has happened to Lars!" Marlotta spoke sharply.

"You need to understand," Bonita addressed Amy. "Aunt Carlotta has gone insane, having to keep herself invisible, hiding out at the club. On drugs all the time. She occasionally poses as Mother just to escape."

"You were a decade younger than us," said Marlotta. "You saw our Hollywood career through rose colored glasses. We were pampered as children. Then the moguls decided Carlotta was the only one of us with true talent. She was chosen for the role of the decade in the defining drama about the French Dixie war. Then they badgered her into the idea that her great performance had to be capped by a self-sacrificial taking of her Death Option to bolster box office receipts. A special retake was set up to kill her. She would be given an Academy Award posthumously."

"We cannot blame her for faking her death," said Bonita. "Or going crazy."

"To add insult to injury the Supreme Court ruled profits had to benefit French war victims. So she wound up a sleazy actress in a time travel scam that sold her sexual favors to the gullible and kinky."

"A sad story," said Amy without emotion. "What about Electra?"

"So you think Carlotta killed Electra?"

"I saw all three triplets together here the night Electra died."

"But you cannot know that Carlotta killed her."

"Even proposing she did, the poor thing is not responsible."

"We have to keep this under wraps, Cousin Amy."

"Amy, we have just tapped the surface with our little sex oriented time travel scenarios here at the club. Great cheering all over the world has greeted the announcement that time travel barriers have been conquered. In the next few years as the industry grows and time travel vacations become more common, especially for the wealthy, our company can emerge as a major player. We can make millions, billions, maybe."

176

"I knew this was all about money." Amy sniffed.

"I mourn for my dear public service minded sister, but we cannot let her passing destroy our business. If the FBI holds us in any way responsible, they will decimate us." Marlotta twisted her ring.

"Cousin Amy, we need you on our side." Bonita smiled a little.

"I intend to be more than just manager of the club."

"Of course! We will make you a partner. You can take Electra's place." Marlotta sounded sincere.

"We are two of a kind." Bonita winked at Amy.

Amy relaxed.

"You are a valuable part of the family. Don't you agree, Mother?"

"Certainly. Now, we know that police captain has been hounding you. Electra was keeping us informed as best she could. What has he discussed with you? Have you told him anything?"

"Nothing he would not find out anyway. He does seem abnormally obsessed with my cat's safety."

"Electra mentioned some foolishness about him talking about a cat witness. But she did not take it seriously."

"I did take my cat to a cat whisperer." Amy's voice was low.

"Nonsense, cats cannot talk to people. That is a scam. The constabulary likes to use such tactics on gullible people to frighten them." Marlotta dismissed the feline frets.

"Do you believe the cat could have talked to the whisperer?"

"Don't be silly, Bonita!"

"No. I didn't expect anything to come of it but I had to take action to help the cat. She was so upset, she was at risk for becoming catatonic." Amy's tone strengthened a little.

"Mother, I'm not so sure animals cannot communicate under some circumstances. There are many things in this world you do not believe in that are real."

"Like vampirism? Really? Grow up, Bonita."

"I'll convince you some day," said Bonita lightly.

"Meanwhile, what do we do about Carlotta?" asked Amy.

"Just leave her to us," Marlotta answered. "I've been dealing with her for years and I know just what to do."

"You worry about the cat. You got her at home, right?" asked Bonita.

"She's missing," said Amy. "She disappeared the same day they found Electra's body."

"You don't think she followed you here?" Bonita's voice held a touch of alarm.

"I don't know where she is." Amy spoke with sadness. "I hope she comes home. I miss her."

Chapter 41

Raize was back at Debriah's front door Sunday morning.

"Officially I'm here to investigate. More overtime. Since her initial account turned out to be true and we found the bodies, I have to interview the cat at once. Personally. Orders from my superiors," he explained. "I complained it is not my expertise but they were adamant."

Debriah arched an eyebrow.

This was going to be interesting.

Shooing him inside, she carried Carousel into the bedroom and deposited her on a pillow.

Raize followed.

As he entered, Debriah positioned herself alongside the feline.

Raize stood with his arms folded, eyeing the still made up bed.

"At least it gives me an excuse to be here today."

"Can you stay all day?"

"My superior has no idea how long it can take to interview a cat. However, I would like to get it done and move on to other pursuits with the cat whisperer. Can you put in a good word for me?" he asked Debriah as he eyed Carousel.

"Go ahead, talk to him," she told the cat.

Raize glanced down at Carousel.

She was looking up at him with wide green eyes.

"Have you anything to say to me?" he asked.

"Meow," she replied.

"According to the Cat Whisperer Professional Association anyone who follows their instructions or takes a few classes for certification can actually talk to cats. Is that true?"

"Meow," said Carousel.

"Well," said Raize. "I am in love with the person who claims quite seriously that she can understand you. So if you are really talking to her, why won't you talk to me?"

Carousel purred loudly.

"It is in your best interest to cooperate. You don't think you had better come clean?"

Carousel bathed her face.

"So that's the way it is. I'm done being nice. You think you can withhold information from the police?"

Purr… Carousel halted her bath. She stood up on the pillow.

"I have ways to make you talk."

"Meow."

"What did she say?"

"Meow," Debriah translated.

"Can't you understand her?"

"Not when she's not talking to me."

"Listen, cat, you are a material witness. I can hold you. How'd you like to bond with the inside of a jail cell?"

"Since the Supreme Court ruled animals do not have Constitutional rights, they cannot be jailed, only impounded with permission of their person or caretaker for medical observation."

Raize glared at Debriah.

"I refuse." Debriah glared back.

Carousel purred again.

"I had to learn basic animal law as a condition of establishing my business," Debriah said.

Carousel stretched and sniffed, settling back down in a comfortable pose.

Raize bounced onto the bed.

"I would still like to know even if she is not talking, can she understand us?"

"I really don't know," Debriah admitted. "Some cats say they can but others vehemently deny it. As truthfulness is not an instinct of felines, we don't know."

"Don't they know truth from lies?"

"Again, not sure. They can report observations and express sensations."

"Would you swear to tell the truth?" Raize asked Carousel.

Carousel closed her eyes.

"This is not working," Raize said to Debriah.

Debriah arched her eyebrow again.

"You don't say."

180

"I do say. I will have to conclude I cannot talk to this cat."

"So why are you trying? I am here." Debriah sniffed.

"I received an order to try myself from my superior. So I can be honest and say that I did so."

"Hmmm."

"How do you do it?" Raize persisted.

"So you do believe in me."

"I just asked a question."

"I cannot explain it. The theory is that during the DNA experiments involving animals and humans at the end of the 21st century somehow the communications skills developed."

"I've heard that idea."

"If you believe that theory." W*hich I don't*, Debriah thought silently. *My ability, like all abilities are gifts from God.*

"How do they explain that?"

"Like in the evolution theory that humans are descended from apes, those of us who can speak with a different species are descended from them."

"So your ancestors were feline?"

"That's the theory."

"But you don't believe it," said Raize perceptively.

"Don't you possess some innate talents you employ as a detective?"

"Maybe. My latest innate talents seem to be getting myself in a jam." Raize reflected silently on his past.

"Harsh. You call being in love with me being in a jam."

They were both now stretched out on the bed, still fully clothed, with Carousel between them.

I don't know if you would love me if you knew I was a Christian, she thought.

I don't know if you would love me if you knew I was a vampire, he thought.

However, he said, "Listen, assuming that cat can talk to you, can she talk to other cat whisperers and testify against us?"

"She would never do that. She's a loving kitty."

"You are saying you trust a cat?"

"Don't you police trust your dogs?"

"We don't talk to them."

"Seriously? You don't employ a dog whisperer on the force? And they are a dime a dozen."

Raize rose from the bed in exasperation.

"Debriah, it cannot be news to you that most people don't believe in talking to animals, much less being linked by DNA. Although supposing that is true, I know some criminals who are antecedents of the rattlesnake. Nevertheless, none of my force is biologically related to dogs."

"It, well, perhaps an anomaly is a better word for my abilities," she said instead. "And I do think you are blessed with intrinsic talents as a detective. At least you can stop crimes like murder."

"I don't know about stopping them but I can usually bring the culprit to justice. There are those who say that it does not matter now that life after death has been proven."

Debriah detected a little satire in his voice.

"Don't you believe in that either?"

"I envision no problem with the official conclusion of the scientific community that there is an afterlife."

"So you believe?"

"I am unsure of what form it will take. What do you think?"

Debriah became more uncomfortable.

"We are getting way off topic. We are supposed to be getting more information from Carousel about the crimes."

"Meow," said Carousel, pleased to be the focus of attention again.

Raize was also happy to abandon the subject.

Discussing beliefs always recalled his past.

His ideas about life and death were intertwined with the vampirist life he had led.

He simply tried not to think about such things in the present.

"I am only officially here to do some work with the feline. I am not supposed to work on you."

He winked at her as he began to unbutton his shirt.

"Carousel wants to cooperate."

"Forget about the cat," he directed.

Carousel jumped to the floor, stalked across the room in a huff, and settled down to watch.

Debriah undressed rapidly.

More slowly he shed his pants, gazing at her.

Debriah watched his actions with rising anticipation. Every inch of his skin exposed made him look better.

He grabbed Debriah and climbed on top of her.

"Good thing I bought a body imprint mattress," Debriah murmured as their bodies blended and the room swayed like a sailboat in a storm.

I wonder if sex like this could bring on a time travel episode, she mused as he vibrated within her and she felt deliciously giddy.

"You are absolutely fantastic."

As he relaxed and rose above her, his clear voice brought her back to reality.

A hear and now reality.

Better than any time travel ever experienced…

Carousel, unnoticed by the couple slipped out of the bedroom, then through the front door. Advancing towards the street, she sniffed the air and started on her way to a different destination.

Chapter 42

"Where is the cat?"

"I told you, she's with that cat whisperer."

Any was scrutinizing the French Dixie war costumed intruder in her home.

The hair color was wrong, but the dark rimmed glasses were a giveaway…

"I've been in hiding, keeping her house under surveillance. The cat left this morning. I tried to follow her but I lost her. Still, I'm sure she came here."

Amy glanced around to see whether Carousel was visible. But to her relief the feline was successfully hiding.

"What do you want with my cat?"

"She knows too much."

"Put down that weapon. Carlotta? Is that you? Where do you imagine you are? In a role-play?"

"I'm living the best part I've ever been cast."

"You are not real. I can do role-play just as well as you. You are no actress."

"I'm not acting."

"You're Marlotta. Your costume is too tight."

The menacing figure suddenly came at her with a silver dagger. Frightened, Amy Raxel slipped her hand into her pocket and activated a smartphone's audio recording app.

"I know you don't have a gun. Too timid to even register as a firearms collector."

"You don't fool me, Marlotta."

"I am not who you think I am. I am Carlotta. I am a great actress!"

"I think you are Marlotta and you are just playing a part to try and scare me!" Amy's identification was becoming less certain.

"I am Carlotta. I cheated the guillotine years ago."

"Doesn't matter, I don't care which one you are, Cousin. I saw you and your clone moving Electra's body after you killed her."

"I am Carlotta! Not that it matters, you'll never talk."

"If you are Carlotta, you must know I came to terms with Marlotta to let me in the business."

"You imagine that means squelch to me? I am going to play out a death scene. Only this time it won't be me taking the Death Option. You are going to commit suicide."

Amy tried to rally and become part of the scene.

"Why, Cousin Carlotta, so it is you. How happy I am that you survived. I perceive we are working on a comeback for you. It- um *The Dixie Wars* was your greatest movie."

Amy's desperation grew as she spoke. She knew she was a poor actress and her dialogue rang false.

The woman in the hoop-skirted dress flashed the dagger so violently that the air around it sounded an alarm.

"You never even saw it. You cannot even remember the name."

"Yes- Yes I can, let's see. Yes, *The Dixie French Sunset* - um, *Gone With the Tornado*, I- uh-"

"You idiot. That was the spoof. The parody."

"Okay, I just need a few seconds to remember. Um, *The French Dixie Dawn?*"

"Forget the stupid movie. You don't know its name. Stop your pathetic patronizing. You saw us both at the club. You know everything."

"I, uh, on the contrary, you hid everything so well. I would never have known that both you and Marlotta were, uh, well, exchanging roles."

"You know everything. Just like my sister saw me kill Lars. She killed that little harlot Watters girl herself."

"Marlotta killed Magdalene Watters after you killed Lars?"

"She was most surprised to behold her husband's girlfriend coming nude down the stairs. It did make her mad."

Amy glanced with alarm at Carousel creeping into the room. "So, uh, why kill me? I'm here to help you."

Carousel ran to the fireplace and hid behind the wood, trying not to get soot in her nostrils. She sneezed.

The killer glanced at the hearth and Amy started forward.

However, she was not quick enough.

"No you don't. You do not want to help me. You just want to expose me. Bring ruin on me and stop my plans."

As her aggressor advanced towards her, Amy altered her tactic. "I may know all about you. But you don't know all about me."

The point of the dagger gleamed as a ray of light bounced off.

"Carlotta, you may be a great actress, but- but I'm a vampire!"

Laughter.

"I am. I am. You cannot kill me. I am one of the undead!" Amy rose up briskly and stood on the sofa, facing down her opponent.

This time she was fast enough that she knew she had caught the other woman off guard.

Amy spread her arms like wings and bared her teeth. A strange light gleamed from her eyes.

She expected Carlotta to cringe. Carlotta, the emotionally high-strung actress would be extremely affected.

Far from being afraid, the woman below her continued laughing as Amy flapped her arms above her head and swooped down.

Then she saw not terror nor emotion in the eyes beholding her, but cool transparency.

Why is she not terrified? Oh! Because-

Gravity abbreviated her conclusion.

In a second, blood spattered everywhere.

Carousel peeked from behind the firewood as the figure in the long dress wiped blood from her face with a draping sleeve.

Then the long slim woman slipped out of the bloodstained garment, allowing it to crumple to the ground partially draping Amy's body. She swiped a blond wig from her head and dropped it on the floor.

"Vampire," the woman laughed again. "That's what you get for giving Bonita such stupid ideas. Bonita fantasizes she's a vampire because of you! That delusion did come in handy when she helped us kill Electra. But that act does not scare me."

She had been nude beneath the voluminous gown and now she

stood completely naked, save for a pair of slippers on her feet. She gingerly picked her way from the center of the dress, careful not to step into the heavy pooling blood so as not to leave footprints. Safely reaching a clean section of the floor, she removed the slippers, tossed them on top of the flared skirt, and tiptoed to the bath.

Carousel shook the ashes from her fur, feeling contaminated, but did not stop to wash as she crept towards the bathroom door.

She could hear the shower running.

Balancing on top of a bookcase, the cat was unprepared for the image emerging from the shower, fully dressed in clothing obviously planted earlier.

The killer had enjoyed a long warm shower, pleased at her success in convincing Amy she was the more famous sister.

Knowing she could convince Amy, she could convince anyone.

She hoped taking her double's identity would not be necessary.

However, it was a valuable strategy to fall back on if ever needed.

The killer was so pleased with herself, she forgot about Carousel until the last minute.

The cat hid on a windowsill behind a curtain as the murderer left the house.

The painful night of the first murders came back to her. Suddenly she understood everything.

Then, comprehending she was too late to offer any comfort, she went to Amy's body and stared.

With new resolve, she left by the cat door a few minutes later, knowing what she had to do next.

Carousel was unaware that the killer had made a dive for her as she slipped through the small square hole in the wall and barely missed grabbing her tail.

She traveled halfway across the city park to her next destination when she finally remembered to stop and bathe.

Chapter 43

At The Men Unadorned Club a female wearing a thick veil turned a key into the lock and entered silently. She had come in the rear entrance.

It was Sunday afternoon and the facility was still shuttered.

The FBI had left the place in a shambles but the building remained intact.

Dancers, gymnasts, and staff had worked diligently to get the club in shape for a reopening this afternoon.

The FBI had taken much of entertainment value from the business. They had searched thoroughly but neglected a large significant part of the premises.

The kitchen.

The completely clean-shaven man met her in the in front of the refrigeration cubicle.

"Hans, you are not performing now. You could wear some clothes, you know."

The man looked puzzled. "I don't have any."

Bonita threw him an apron.

"Listen, I'm sorry about mistaking that one middle-aged woman for the one I was supposed to hook up with. They looked alike."

"I don't understand how you saw that. I didn't think my aunts looked anything like each other."

"I'm just grateful your mother did not fire me when that spy took my place."

"We took care of that problem. We're suing him. And, despite having to use the cop instead of you, the objective of that scene was executed anyway, yielding the same result, as you are about to see."

"I would have enjoyed it. Back when I was in the military, I-"

"I don't want to know any of the details of your former life. Just proceed with the mummification. The Egyptian costume is in a box on the table. The creature has to look like a wax figure and no older than 36 when you finish, understand?"

"Perfectly. I have an embalming certificate and a Master of

Mummification. Not to mention an Associate in Artistry of Makeup."

"Great. The glass domed coffin will be delivered before you finish."

The hairless man opened the freezer chest and began working on the corpse of Carlotta Fortune.

Bonita left the kitchen and waited at the front entrance.

She anticipated the other man she sought after would be bringing the display. The red haired man with the sharp beard, fully clothed, arrived on schedule with the box and she helped him wheel it into the kitchen, where the first man was absorbed in his work.

"Are you the new manager?" he asked in a friendly tone.

"Can you give me a private performance?" Bonita asked the red headed man.

"Of course." He started taking his shirt off.

"Come here," she said enticingly. "Back to my private quarters."

"Is the club still going to host the activities in the hidden places? I assumed that all was canceled with all the cops around after the murders. I never got a chance to participate."

"Did you want to?"

"I heard it was a lot more money. But no more French Dixie activities. No playacting by Carlotta Fortune. Won't that cut into profits?"

"Oh, the club is going to prepare a new attraction. A type of a wax museum. We're still going to use Aunt Carlotta's image. Along with other interesting persons. Come this way with me."

"Cool."

She led him down the hall to the theatre setting.

Bonita was eager to make an impression on her mother and Marlotta's extended absence presented a golden opportunity. She knew her mother would have to hide until the furor over the multiple fatalities and disappearances died down.

If it did.

Bonita knew where her mother had gone and knew what her mission entailed.

Ensuring, if necessary, Marlotta Holt could pass as her sister

189

Carlotta, since that body had never been found.

And never would be.

Bonita was mildly disappointed not to be helping Marlotta. However, she had planned some compensation for herself.

And she could not be in two places at the same time.

It must have been awfully convenient to have a secret clone-like sister dependent on you.

"Can't have everything," Bonita spoke aloud.

"What can't you have?" The man paused as they began to enter.

"An Army career, for one thing. On the other hand, I have you."

Bonita smiled.

"You know, I'm sure you are under 30. I don't want to do anything against the law." The man hesitated.

"I'll sign a release. The forms are in the desk."

"Is that allowed?"

"Oh yes. Undoubtedly permitted. Top drawer."

As he bent over the desk drawer, she grabbed his arms and pinned him down. Within minutes she bound him with straps.

"Hey, what's the idea?"

"I'm more than the new manager, I'm the new owner," she revealed. "My biological age makes no difference. Aunt Carlotta needs slaves."

"What?"

Bonita removed the fake rounded teeth.

"You are beginning your training for exotic role playing time travel," she informed him. "Prepare to fly!"

She pushed him down on the soft bed and she sprang on top of him.

He screamed when her teeth sank into his neck.

Chapter 44

"Carousel has vanished again!"

Raize and Debriah had fallen asleep.

Dark had fallen.

Fear woke Debriah shortly after 1 AM Monday.

She checked on Raize. He breathed rhythmically, sleeping soundly in her bed.

She hunted for Carousel but no kitty was in evidence.

She woke Raize up.

"Oh, the cat is probably out prowling," he complained. "Let me go back to sleep."

The police captain's cellphone sounded.

A middle of the night call.

No more sleep tonight.

Raize listened grimly, then hung up and addressed Debriah.

"They found another body."

"Oh no! Don't tell me! Not Carousel!"

"No, thank goodness, only a human being this time."

"Don't be sarcastic. I'm still worried sick about Carousel."

Raize started to get up and get dressed.

"Who else is dead?"

"Amy Raxel."

Monday evening arrived before Raize got back to Debriah. He had sworn her to secrecy about Carousel's latest vanishing act but permitted her to embark on a physical search of the neighborhood during the daylight.

Debriah went all over the subdivision calling 'kitty, kitty, kitty'.

She did so in vain.

By the time Raize returned, she was exhausted and discouraged and already dressed for bed.

Keeping his clothes on, Raize dropped down on the couch with her.

"Carousel is still gone. And now another casualty? Everything is going wrong, isn't it?"

"Don't give up. We now know more than ever. We just cannot prove anything. But there will be closure soon."

"Because Amy Raxel has been killed?"

"Yes."

"How? Is her death going lead to justice for Lars Holt and Magdalene Rene Watters?"

"Partial justice, at least. We found Electra's smartphone on Amy Raxel's body. It was set to record. It picked up the entire audio of the killing."

"And the killer never saw it?"

"The billowy dress the murderer shed covered it. So she missed it."

"What does it say?"

"Your psychic prediction was spot on. On the device the murderer identifies herself as Carlotta, telling Amy she must die because she witnessed the identical sisters with Electra's dead body at the club."

"So they killed Electra?"

"Probably. The killer then reveals she killed Lars, her brother-in-law, and then called Marlotta over to help move the body. When Marlotta arrived, Magdalene Rene came down the stairs nude and Marlotta, immediately jumping to the correct conclusion that this was her husband's lover, did the honors that time. Together they disposed of those bodies. Amy's killer told her this story with satisfaction unaware she was being recorded."

"Where would Amy get Electra's smartphone?"

"Remember she was found with Electra's body and was suspected of being her killer for a short time. On the recording Amy accuses Marlotta and Carlotta of killing Electra. But apparently she walked into the scene after Electra was already dead."

"So you don't know who actually killed her."

"One of them had to. And then, if Amy was telling the truth, the same culprit killed her last sister. And now Marlotta Holt, or Carlotta Fortune- I'm just saying Marlotta from now on for brevity and clarity- is wanted for questioning. But she's nowhere to be found.

Carlotta, allowing she is real, has vanished into thin air just like that from whence she came. It is hard to track someone who is part of a mirror image team where legally only one has existed for years."

"That's why Carousel was so confused. Being identical, I suppose their scents are hard to distinguish."

"We don't know which one was on the tape. Amy was not sure. As it was happening, she accused her killer of being both. The killer insisted she was Carlotta, but I don't believe it."

"Don't we know at least one of them is dead?"

"We only have Loyce's account. Remember he was drugged. If he woke up next to one of them, she may not have been dead."

"Is it possible there was only one all along? Carlotta may have not died in *Twilight of the French South* but are we sure she had been here all along?"

"No. But I think Marlotta was the stronger, and if one of them is dead, it's Carlotta. Analysis of a body would tell which of them it was, since one gave birth and the other was childless. It seems that the only person left alive who could tell them apart is Bonita."

"And where do you think Marlotta is?"

"Hidden somewhere. Bonita is shielding Marlotta, I guess. Most likely Bonita was unaware her mother's mirror image was still around, might still be in the dark."

"But why kill your identical sister? Surely she was useful to her."

"To take her place and leave her the blame for it all."

"And why kill Electra? Was she really the third sister?"

"We're still working that out. But if true, Electra also could tell Marlotta and Carlotta apart. Amy and Electra could have testified that Carlotta was not dead all these many years in a fraud trial. Possibly Lars Holt knew. We don't know. Maybe not. Remember the life insurance paid so many years ago. Insurance companies never forget or forgive. That's motive."

"Who else might know?"

"Just Bonita. Since Bonita is Marlotta's daughter, that is another clue that Marlotta is still alive. Bonita is unafraid. That implicates Marlotta."

"Yes. Carlotta would kill her niece but Marlotta would not kill her daughter? Maybe Bonita will cooperate now that her mother is missing."

"She has been defiant so far. She's playing the age harassment card every time we talk to her."

"You think Bonita knows everything now? What does she tell you?"

"She says her mother is not unaccounted for, just temporarily gone and will return soon. She claims Carlotta Fortune died at the end of *Twilight of the French South* and her other aunt has not been heard from in years. Loyce Landers was participating in a voluntary work related role-play, was inadvertently abandoned, and at the most has a civil case for neglect. The police are making all this up to harass the club because an FBI agent's corpse happen to be dumped there after a killing totally unconnected to the location."

"And her father's death?"

"Killed by burglars. Or the Watters couple for messing with Magdalene."

"Oh, how can she get away with such atrocious allegations?"

"Because we have no proof. She is accusing me of making biased insinuations."

"She hasn't been told about the smartphone recording?"

"Of course not. I am trying to preempt any preposterous theory that it was a role-play reenactment cloaking Amy's suicide."

"What do you think led to Lars and Magdalene's murders?"

"Our premise now that we have heard the smartphone recording is that Lars Holt's affair with Magdalene put the whole lucrative setup at risk. Assuming the recording is to be believed, Carlotta recognized this and killed him, starting a deadly chain of events."

"Is that the idea? Will all this stand up in court should you catch Marlotta?"

"Weak. I admit it but we only have what we have. We cannot prove anything. Right now we are first trying to prove that Electra was the third sister. We only have Amy's statement to me. And now she's been silenced."

"We still have the fashion dolls. And I propose the dolls prove it. With the dolls we can illustrate Electra was the third triplet."

"How?"

"Can you procure a photo of your deceased coworker?"

"Somehow."

"Then I can use portraiture forensics to show the third doll is based on Electra."

"Sounds good but the fashion dolls are not that much help. Someone will claim they are reproductions, fabricated recently to back up what we conclude. And how do you know they are not?"

"We can get them authenticated by an expert to banish your doubts. They are never removed from box condition!"

"I still fail to comprehend how that helps us. Even if we catch one or both of them, we cannot conclusively prove which one is the killer. But we can send someone to jail as an accessory and or conspirator. That will be some small accomplishment."

"Well, I'm exhausted. Let's go to bed."

"I can't stay tonight. I have to go back to the office soon and meet with the FBI again. They require a report on Amy's murder."

"Oh." Debriah quickly re-energized. He might not be back for a long time. She shed her nightgown.

Cutting the light off at the wall switch, he undressed rapidly.

The moonlight beamed into her den windows.

She loved the way all his hair grew perfectly symmetrical, framing him with the effect of an exquisite tattoo, only subtle and silky.

She began tracing the outline of this artwork… He grabbed her and pulled her down on the sofa, kissing her with passion…

Expressing their love on the couch, neither heard the key turn in the front door.

"I got off a little early and decided I would drop by and model my wedding gown for you." Samantha's voice called out, almost singing as she burst into Debriah's house.

She flipped on the den light and dropped a voluminous garment bag.

Only then seeing Debriah and Raize entangled nude on the

195

sofa.

Raize jumped up abruptly and Debriah dived for cover under the cushions.

Samantha gulped as her eyes were drawn to Raize's near perfect form. Reaching for his clothing, his movements demonstrated a combination of grace and power.

Debriah merely gathered the cushions around her.

Raize dressed as quickly as he had undressed.

"Since you dropped by, it saves me a trip to your place. I require the records of your conversations with Amy Raxel," he told Samantha.

"I gave you that information in true confidence! If I give you the records, I could lose my license!"

"Not anymore. An intruder murdered her a few hours ago."

Someone else who suspected you are a vampire now murdered. An unbidden thought.

A little chill rippled through Samantha.

"How did she die?"

"A silver dagger through the heart."

Debriah's throat tightened at Samantha's expression.

Then the cat whisperer relaxed.

This was Raize, the man she loved.

And I trust him! she told herself fiercely.

Chapter 45

"I would anticipate you would trust my judgment after all these years."

"My dear, I did not know."

Mr. Watters put his arm around his wife. He was trembling.

She was calm.

"Naturally you didn't. You were always allergic to cats. So how could I tell you?"

"But I feel as though I have denied you feline relationships for over 50 years. You must resent it."

"Nonsense. Just because I understand the kitties does not mean I have to have lots of them about or even just one live with me. It's a gift. Most of us don't ever even practice it. I did belong to a little unofficial group in college but I gave it up for you. It was just child's play back then anyway."

"You really can talk to cats. You are a cat whisperer just like that Debriah Brock. All these years and I'm still finding out secrets about you. I'm amazed."

"We did not call it cat whisperer back then," she murmured as she scratched Carousel's neck. "Just talking to cats for fun."

Mr. Watters took another dose of his allergy medication. He also placed some menthol salve under his nose. He had stocked up a lifetime supply before the latter was outlawed several years ago.

"How did that cat know to come tell you who murdered our granddaughter?"

"Cats just know who can understand them, dear."

"And did you? I mean, which of you...?" His words faded gradually.

Carousel and Mrs. Watters exchanged glances.

"I am confident you do not want to know the details. Believe me if I had not needed your help to bury her, I would not have troubled you at all."

Mr. Watters picked up the shovel. "I still think it would have been simpler if I had just shot her."

Mrs. Watters cleared her throat.

"I see the kitty has already scratched quite a hole in the ground." Mr. Watters started to dig in the same spot.

"I do know Ms. Raxel also had a beloved puppy. I heard he escaped from the adoption shelter. He's possibly spent some time with the Pomeranian next door, so it worked out that he came to her."

"An escapee dog? They will recapture him! What if he talks?"

"Nobody believes canine whisperers, dear. That profession is riddled with fraud."

"Hmmm."

"And if you had shot this creature you might be taken to prison. As it is, all you are doing is digging a hole. No blame can attach to you."

Mr. Watters dug faster, fleshing out the indention in his backyard to make it deeper and wider, more even at the edges.

"Good thing we are having the patio put in next week."

"True. It all worked out so well. Carousel told me who killed our Magdalene Rene and, just a few hours later, this same abomination comes knocking on the door, pretending to search for her lost cat. It was Providence, no doubt."

He paused. "You don't think, well, I know there is an afterlife. You don't fear that this might have been wrong."

Carousel hissed.

"We loved our granddaughter," said Mrs. Watters simply. "Didn't we? We went through so much to keep her. So many age reduction petitions. All that paperwork in vain."

Carousel hissed again, sniffing at the body of Marlotta Holt.

"We loved her enough to pass her off as our granddaughter, rather than our great-granddaughter. We don't have to worry about that anymore. You're right. We loved her enough to risk jail."

"Just like this kitty loved her mistress. Cats are very loyal."

"Yes." Mr. Watters stared at the long slits on the arms of the dead woman. "She must possess extremely sharp claws. You don't fear it was wrong to aid and abet her cover up."

"Meow," said Carousel.

A little guilt for letting Carousel take all the blame aggravated Mrs. Watters, but her husband was so old fashioned about killing.

198

"Now, Earl, we are in our 120s. Carousel is only about four. Her life is all ahead of her. She deserves not be always looking over her shoulder, wondering when the law will catch up with her."

"So we let her escape all consequences for this death?"

Carousel's eyes narrowed as she surveyed Mr. Watters.

"This woman murdered our Magdalene. Not to mention Carousel suspects she conspired to kill or did kill several others."

Carousel kept her gaze on the man as Mrs. Watters scratched her tail.

"Yes, well, I suppose you are right. Carousel, you run along home now." Mr. Watters spoke somewhat shakily as Carousel spread her claws.

He resumed shoveling.

"She needs a lift. Her new home is nowhere near here. You do need a lift, don't you?"

Carousel nodded. Her new mistress, Debriah Brock, resided quite a distance away.

Mr. Watters finally finished his chore, still appearing depressed. They prepared to leave.

"That's that." Mrs. Watters dusted her hands. "We lost our descendants. And it is understandable to be sad. But we will see them again. We are still healthy and free. Life is worth living. As soon as we get back, dear, I propose it will be an occasion for ice cream."

Mr. Watters perked up, then glanced around nervously. "Not so loud."

"Sorry. I made a batch the other night. Very quietly."

Mrs. Watters still kept her forbidden ice cream maker and was old enough to remember how to use it.

"Where did you get the cream?"

"Oh, don't ask so many questions, dear. Just dig." Mrs. Watters stretched her short plump fingers in front of her, peering at her hands.

For just a moment, she fancied instead of perfect pink fingernails, there were ten retractable claws…

Chapter 46

"I hope there are no more bodies to be found anytime soon,"

After spending the day at the office filing papers to categorize the case dormant, Raize was back at Debriah's house Tuesday night.

He rejected meeting at the library, which was now back in business.

"We need to keep our social contacts there for the future." Debriah peered at her calendar hanging on the wall and raised a pen.

"Agreed. Your reading activities and my being a regular bed renter gives us much needed wholesome cover. But we are safe here for tonight."

"Before I go back, I'm going to try to register as a voice actor so I can read to people who might actually hear me," said Debriah.

This ambition failed to penetrate Raize's radar.

"Marlotta and Carlotta are still out there. There is still no concrete evidence that one of them is dead," he continued, his eyes locked in a far off stare. "Even if so, I don't want to view any more corpses tonight. As far as I care, the duplicate Fortune sisters can stay vanished forever. I need some rest. I have to be at work early in the morning."

"Just so long as Carousel comes back. I'm so worried about her." Debriah turned her back on the wall hanging.

"She's okay. Stop worrying." Raize's look became vague.

"That's what you kept saying about Loyce."

"And I was right. He's fine. Let's enjoy a stress free evening. You did take away Samantha's house key?" He now glared, sharply flipping his train of thought.

"Yes. I did. And I just marked the upcoming days we have free."

"I hope she understood. Shall we eat first? I'll conjure up something to cook."

She will be understanding when I do ask for the key back, Debriah hoped silently.

"I can guarantee you Samantha will not be here tonight. She's with Loyce."

"Thank God," said Raize. "Alone at last. Dinner and romance in impenetrable privacy."

Not even the cat will bother us tonight. He grinned as he opened the refrigerator. He pretended he was coming into the bedroom with food. Debriah paid scant attention as he placed a bag before her.

"What did you bring us to eat?" she asked.

"Open the bag."

Debriah grabbed the bag and pulled out two long narrow boxes.

She gasped.

Expertly carved identical faces stared up at her. Marlotta and Carlotta as fashion dolls.

"How did you get them? You saved them from destruction!"

"I sent word those dolls were pertinent to the investigation and snatched them out of the destruction bin. Now, you have to keep them hidden. But I suspect no one will ever remember they exist."

Debriah turned the boxes in the lamplight.

"Thank you, Raize. You are wonderful! I love you!"

Across town, a luxury car exited a driveway and headed towards the domicile of Debriah Brock.

Enjoying the smooth ride, Carousel bathed contentedly in the passenger seat of Mrs. Watters' Pacifica.

Mr. Watters rested in the backseat.

Mrs. Watters hummed old the old Christian hymn, *Peace in the Valley* softly, as she drove.

Evocative lights of the city rhythmically sparkling,

Headlights from cars like blinking diamonds.

The moon glowed brightly and stars competed for space.

Debriah and Raize had ingested a light dinner in the bedroom. The noise from wheels slowing on pavement alerted the couple. Debriah froze. Raize grabbed his gun.

The Pacifica halted in the driveway.

Skittish, more afraid of discovery than mayhem, Raize hid in the closet, directing Debriah to procure her own firearm.

The doorbell sounded.

Debriah reacted to Raize's instruction with disobedience due to a total lack of misgivings.

Her instincts assured her that no enemy loomed at the door. She did stash her new dolls under the bed before proceeding to the den.

She squinted through the peephole and relaxed.

Opening her front door wide, Debriah was surprised and pleased when an elderly lady deposited the purring cat in her arms.

"I have no idea how she had gotten lost again! I was so worried! Carousel, you know I'm your new mistress! It's official! You know this is your territory now. No more roaming!"

Carousel met her new person's eyes and blinked.

"I do think this kitty might be a wanderer," Mrs. Watters warned, after briefly introducing herself in a whispery tone.

"I'm afraid so."

"A good thing you put a tag with your name and address on her collar. Maybe someday those traceable chips will be legal again on animals just like they are on people now."

"Thank you so much for finding her. I am so grateful."

"Not at all," said Mrs. Watters.

"Would you like to come in?"

A sharp angry noise sounded from the bedroom.

"No, my dear, thank you. It's way beyond time my husband and I got back home. He's allergic so his pills are making him sleepy."

Having moved up to the passenger seat, Mr. Watters was sipping melted ice cream disguised in a coffee cup.

"Again, thank you so much."

"Farewell, Carousel. You be a good kitty, now."

And if Debriah saw the wink that passed between the elderly lady and the feline as they parted, she gave no indication.

"Where has that cat been and what has she been up to?" Raize demanded as he appeared, having left the closet a bit prematurely.

Carousel bounded around him, paying him no notice.

The feline switched her tail and then wrapped it around her

paws as she settled on the bed. She looked demurely to the side.

Debriah gave the cat a sly glance.

She knew better than to ask.

"Did you know that woman?" Raize asked.

"Never saw her before."

"Hmm, I feel a sense of familiarity, listening from the closet. Never mind, time is fleeting, my love." He gestured grandly.

Debriah followed his guidance.

So did Carousel.

"Does she have to follow us into the bedroom?"

"She preceded me in, and you were already here, if you want to get technical."

The feline perched on the headboard, resuming her bath. She began diligently cleaning her claws.

The man and woman were completely nude and playing on the bed in seconds.

"I hope you know she can blackmail us now." Raize laughed.

"She would never to that, would you, Carousel?"

Carousel batted her luscious eyelashes. The meow she gave out was incredibly discreet although an intense light shined in her eyes. She flexed her claws.

Raize took hold of Debriah.

There was no more conversation.

Stretching and grasping amidst the sheets, Raize and Debriah forgot the watching feline as their teeth found flesh.

Published by Ruskras Corner

Science Fiction-*Karl Sabers Space Knight Adventures* - by Carl S. Kralich

3748 A.D. The Return of the Cat

Auction of Worlds

"Humorous young adult science fiction. Hilarious tale of princesses, pirates and a talking cat. For adults and young adults, male and female. Romance and gallantry in the stars."

Historical Literature Fiction by Deborah DR Kralich

The Mystery of the Missing Persons - set in the 1960s

The turbulent 60s viewed from the eyes of a child who is writing her first mystery book.

Historical Murder Mysteries-by Deborah DR Kralich

The Mystique Woven in Our Land – set in 1792

The unlikely combination of witchcraft and high treason lead to treachery and murder haunting a hero's daughter and the soldier she loves.

Murder as the Organist Plays – set in 1904

As the wedding music starts, the bride begins her long walk to the arms of her groom. But she will not finish the journey. The beautiful bride emerges stunned, blood on her dress. She stands alone, blood dripping from a dagger at her fingertips. Unknowing, his back to this scenario, the organist plays on...

Lt. Plate in Sand Waves Mysteries– A series of traditional mysteries set in the 1980s including:

An Innovative Murder for the Season

At a small specialty store in a high-income community, a dozen or so people are trapped for 3 days and 2 nights. On the surface most appear to be strangers caught at random. Then there is a murder and it turns out the only real stranger among them is a detective whose presence is hardly coincidental.

The Ruler of the Toys

Intolerance and prejudice are major factors in the murder of an innocent woman who should have been without an enemy in the world. Before he can expose the masquerade of the killer, Lt. Plate has to uncover and understand deep dark secrets of long vanished eras.

A Kaleidoscope of Masquerades

Climatic events at a 1983 masquerade ball are merely the beginning of a kaleidoscope of confusion and anarchy that threatens life and liberty of a society facing change and choices that will reverberate into the future known as now.

The Unknown Puppeteer

On the eve of their marriage, Lt. Plate and Daphne must uncover a ruthless murderer or forfeit their chance for happiness for all time.

Interlude of Carelessness- set in the 1930s

Romance, intrigue, and mystery on the eve of World War II

Available on Amazon and Kindle